Life Pushes You Along

By

Emma Sterner-Radley

Life Pushes You Along

Published by Heartsome Publishing
Ivory Close, Staffordshire, ST1 3GG, United Kingdom
www.heartsomebooks.com

First Heartsome edition: May 2017

Emma Sterner-Radley asserts the moral right to be identified as the author of this work.

DEDICATION

To Amanda

For showing the ultimate sign of love – fighting harder for my dreams than her own.

And to Malin

For building the framework that made me into the author I am today.

ACKNOWLEDGEMENTS

Firstly, I have to thank my family for always being supportive no matter what craziness I decide to do with my life. Mamma, pappa, Anna, Torbjörn, Oscar, Victor, Ester. You are so patient and loving and I am proud to be your daughter, sister and aunt. I cannot thank you enough.

Secondly, thank you to the woman who helps me, pushes me, worries about me and makes my life unmeasurably better just by being in it, My darling wife. Amanda – without you I never would have gotten to where I am now. I will spend the rest of our lives together trying to repay you with the same sort of love and care that you show me. You're my miracle.

Thirdly, I have to thank the three women who helped create this book. First, a great writer who agreed to beta read this book – Angela Brooks. Thank you so much and do let me know when I can return the favour! Then we have the two editors. Thank you to Frances Moloney and a particularly heartfelt thank you to Cheri Fuller who went above and beyond!

Finally, we come to a more sombre acknowledgment.

I need to thank a person that I wish everyone could have met. If you had, I'm sure she would have made you a better person like she did me. She was my sister, my confidant and my moral compass. Malin, I'm sorry that I wasn't there when you needed me. I'm sorry that I can never show you that you were right to be proud of me. And I'm sorry that this book comes out with my name on the spine, when yours is the one that people should remember. With that in mind, I will at least put your name in this book for any of my readers to see.

Jag älskar dig. Jag saknar dig.

Och jag kommer aldrig att låta dig bli bortglömd

Malin Sterner
1973-2011

CHAPTER ONE

Zoe

Zoe watched as one of her favourite customers observed her with what seemed to be desperation. She felt her heart twinge with sympathy.

"So, do you have it?" he asked.

She knew she was going to disappoint him.

"I'm not sure, Mr. Evans. A book with a bird on the cover that was based somewhere with a big forest… that doesn't ring a bell, I'm afraid."

The bookshop's unpleasantly sharp fluorescent lights showed every crease on his wrinkled face as it took on an embarrassed look.

Zoe quickly added, "I know the feeling though. There's lots of books I have been looking for and I can't remember anything but the cover, or a piece of the plot, or half of the author's name. It's a pain."

He nodded. "Yes. Yes, my dear, it certainly is."

"Do you remember anything else about the book? Who was the main character?"

He looked up at the ceiling for a moment. "I suppose she was quite a bit like you, actually."

Zoe felt her brow furrowing. She didn't want to be rude but that didn't narrow it down much. Did he, perhaps, mean that the main character was someone who worked with customers, someone who dressed like her, or someone who was in their late twenties? She hoped he wasn't alluding to the fact that she wasn't white because she wasn't sure if a conversation with this elderly gentleman would stay politically correct if they got onto that subject. She liked Mr. Evans and wanted to continue liking him.

"I see. Um, how was she like me?"

"Young and likable," he answered simply.

Zoe was relieved. It was still just as impossible to find the book he was looking for, though.

"I'm afraid that doesn't give me much to go on. Tell you what, I'll keep an eye out for a book with a forest setting and a bird on the cover. We have your contact details on file, so I can call you if we get it in?"

His face lit up. "That would be splendid! Thank you ever so much for your help."

She smiled at him, happy to be able to help. Mr. Evans put his trilby hat back on, and she couldn't help but smile at his posh, old-fashioned sense of style which perfectly matched his way of speaking.

"Goodbye. I hope to hear from you but if I do not, I shall come in to purchase another book instead."

"You do that, Mr. Evans. Goodbye."

Just as he was leaving the bookshop, he turned around and shouted, "Oh, by the way, it might have been something other than a bird, now that I think about it. I think it was something that flew. So, maybe t'was a bat, a moth, or perhaps a ferret? Anyway, cheerio."

The door closed behind him and Zoe stared into space, puzzled.

Had he meant to say 'ferret'? How the hell was that categorized as something that flew?

Zoe's manager, and the owner of the bookshop, Darren, walked in with a small box under one arm.

He held out the box to her. "We've got a book delivery. Who was that?" He inclined his head towards the door.

"Oh, it was Mr. Evans."

Darren's bushy eyebrows met at the bridge of his nose. "Who?"

"Mr. Evans. You know, the retired bank manager who likes books about nature and sea journeys. Comes in here every week?"

Darren still looked like he was trying to do complicated arithmetic.

Zoe managed not to sigh. "The old guy with the big mole on his right cheek?"

"Oh, that crazy, posh old badger. Right. Anyway, here's the new batch. Put them on the system and then shelve them, will you?"

She gave a curt nod and took the box from him. There was no reason why he couldn't do this himself–well there was one reason and that was simply that he was lazy. He'd stand at the counter and watch her put the books out, and as soon as she was done he'd slink back into the breakroom, leaving her to man the counter as always, while he drank his bodyweight in sweet tea. No wonder he always needs to use the loo, she thought as she unpacked the books. She put them on the system and looked at the packing slip to check the details as she did so.

Her job wasn't the dream that most other book-nerds conjured up when she told them what she did. Yes, she worked in an independent bookshop. However, it was a lacklustre bookshop, where she was overworked, her boss didn't care much about the running of the place, and the clientele was dwindling.

As Zoe began to shelve the books, she looked around at the cheap birch bookcases, faded beige walls, and harsh fluorescent lights and thought about how she had ended up here.

She had been in dire straits when she applied for this job. She had been out on the street since her parents kicked her out. She didn't think she was focused enough for further education, she was down to her last twenty pounds and totally unqualified for any job.

Out of desperation, she had applied for this position and when Darren had asked her, in the interview, why he should hire her and not the other two applicants, who both had degrees and experience, she had broken down in tears. He had grumbled about not being able to stand seeing people cry and after a long chat about her situation, he had agreed to give her the job on a trial basis. She had never known how to thank him for that, and so she merely put up with him as a way of showing her gratitude.

She had just turned eighteen back then and she had stayed in the job for the following eight years out of loyalty, habit, and a feeling that there was no other job out there for her.

She sighed as she placed another book on the shelf. What was she qualified to do? Other bookshops were run a lot more professionally than Darren's Book Nook. Her quick foray into wanted-ads told her that they would demand that she "showed initiative" and "managed her own workload." She was sure she wasn't ready for that. She figured that a trained monkey could do the job she was doing right now and so that was what she would stick with, no matter how much it bored her.

The little bell above the door rang out. Before Zoe had time to turn to see who their new customer was, she heard Darren's sharp intake of breath. She knew immediately who must be at the door. Rebecca Clare.

Their favourite customer was shaking drops of water from her elegant brown coat and looked unfairly beautiful despite her red hair being wet and her glasses covered in little raindrops. Zoe stole as many glances as she dared while Rebecca rid herself of the worst of the rain. She admired the fancy high-heeled shoes, the black stockings, and what she could see of the knee-length black dress under her coat. And that was saying nothing about her face; those stunning eyes and the heart-shaped lips were truly mesmerizing. Especially this close up. Rebecca was near enough for Zoe to be able to reach out and brush her cheek. Not that she was daydreaming about that, of course.

Zoe knew she shouldn't be staring. Not only because it was rude, and borderline objectifying, but because Rebecca was way out of her league. And far too old for her. Zoe didn't know how old Rebecca was but she was certainly older than her own twenty-six years. Oh, and to make Rebecca even more of an impossible choice, she was Darren's huge crush too.

Just as Zoe was dragging her gaze away, she saw Rebecca quickly remove her drenched glasses. The water that had rested on them shot out in Zoe's direction, some hitting the side of her face.

Rebecca looked mortified. "Oh, I'm so sorry. Are you all right, there?"

"Yeah, sure! I'm, uh, waterproof," Zoe replied. She hoped her tone was light and jokey but worried that she sounded as terrified as she always felt when this woman spoke to her.

They had never had any long conversations, she realised. Zoe, and by extension, Darren, only knew Rebecca's name because she had ordered books and they always took contact information to be able to call or e-mail the customer when their book arrived. Rebecca Clare, RebeccaClare@acacia-recruitment.com, Zoe repeated in her head, stopping herself before she reeled off the memorized phone number too.

The contact information, which showed that she must work in recruitment considering the company's name, and Rebecca's fondness for crime-fiction was all Zoe knew about this woman. Well, that and the fact that she had the sort of presence that you couldn't miss. Despite Rebecca's feminine looks and apparel, there was almost a masculine air to her behaviour. Zoe realised that what she saw as masculine could probably be boiled down to confidence, calm, directness, and a sense of power. Rebecca was polite and friendly but in a way that spoke of a person who you couldn't take for granted.

Either way, Rebecca Clare demanded all the attention of her onlookers without having to fight for it. And that, combined with her obvious beauty, took Zoe's breath away. Just as it was doing right now as she stood with droplets of water running down her cheek and Rebecca smiling politely at her.

Zoe wiped away the water from her face with her sweater sleeve and watched Rebecca dry her glasses on a tissue she had taken out of her pocket. Then she put the glasses back on. Zoe struggled to find something to say. Something normal. Something witty.

She heard Darren clear his throat and come rushing over.

"Mrs. Clare, isn't it? Come to pick up your latest bloodcurdling chiller?" He grinned at Rebecca. Zoe realised that he probably thought it was a charming smirk. It wasn't.

"It's Ms. Clare," Rebecca replied casually. "And yes, please. I got an email a few days ago and haven't had time to pop in until today."

"Terrible weather for it, though. You should have waited until tomorrow," Darren said, his strange smile still fixed in place.

Zoe saw Rebecca raise an eyebrow for a brief moment.

"Well, it's meant to rain all week, so planning to only go out when it's dry seems futile. We're Londoners, right? We're experts at dealing with rain."

Darren laughed, far too loudly and for far too long. Zoe wondered if Rebecca was suffering from second-hand embarrassment as much as she was right now. Deciding to rescue the other woman, Zoe put the books down and went behind the counter to pick up the book Rebecca had ordered and put it through the till.

When she was done, she handed Rebecca the thick tome. "Here's your book. I've never heard of this author. Is she any good?"

"Very good. Or, at least, her last three books have been. Here's hoping her latest doesn't disappoint." Rebecca looked down at the book and gave the front cover a quick pat. Then she looked back up at Zoe, with a smile.

Zoe felt herself freeze. She was meant to be telling Rebecca the total for the book, and asking if she wanted a bag but all she could do was stare. The charming smile was bad enough but Zoe had just ignored her own advice – never look this woman in the eye.

Rebecca Clare's eyes were a common blue-green colour, but what made them so dangerous was that they always seemed to glimmer. As if Rebecca was constantly happy. Or constantly flirting. It was insanely distracting and Zoe had to force herself to ignore those gorgeous eyes and just say the total sum. She barely remembered to offer a bag for the book.

When Rebecca had paid and thanked her, she turned on her high heels and click-clacked back out into the rain and out of Zoe's line of vision. Zoe sighed deeply and stopped herself when she realised that Darren could probably hear her.

It turned out that she didn't need to worry about that. Darren was busy staring after Rebecca, looking like an abandoned puppy. Zoe looked around at the shop which suddenly looked ten times duller and knew how he felt.

CHAPTER TWO

Zoe

Zoe could have been at her local library already. It was a Sunday and going to the library was her only plan since she didn't have to go into Central London to work today.

Instead, she was sitting in a café listening to her brother, Jamie, talk about the woman he was dating. That wouldn't have been a problem if it wasn't for the fact that the woman in question was Zoe's best friend, Helen. Hearing about how happy the two of them were made Zoe feel a bit queasy. Somehow it felt weird to think that the girl she had known since she was seven was now dating her brother – the guy they had always thought was dumb and weird, especially when he put pebbles in their lunchboxes.

Queasy or not, here she was. Queenswell Library, cool and quiet, was calling her name and she was stuck drinking bad coffee and listening to Jamie talk about how "Helen always knew what he was thinking". She fought back a yawn.

"Christ, Zoe. Could you look anymore bored?" Jamie asked.

"I could try. Would you like me to try?"

"No. I'd like you to make an effort and pretend that you're happy for your older brother."

"I am happy. I'm ecstatic. I'm painting the world with rainbows."

He scoffed into his latte. "Yeah, you are but that's just because you're hella gay."

"Really? 'Hella gay?' Is that what we are calling my sexuality now? You're twenty-eight, you're too old to be using words like 'hella'."

Jamie put his cup down. "Okay. What's wrong, grumpy guts?"

"Nothing. I'm sorry. I'm just… having some sort of existential crisis, I think."

"Pardon?"

"I'm sick of my job and I'm sick of being single and I'm sick of… me."

"Well, we're all sick of you but there's nothing to be done about that, I'm afraid. I checked," he joked.

She picked up a small bag of sweetener, fidgeted with it, and then shoved it back into its holder. "Yeah? With whom? Mum and Dad?"

The banter died in its tracks. Jamie looked as though she had slapped him.

"You know I don't talk to them about you. I check in with them occasionally to make sure they aren't dead, but that is as far as it goes. You know I have no patience for them and their bloody homophobia."

"I know. I'm sorry. I didn't mean to bring them up. Ignore me. I'm just in a weird mood lately."

"You're telling me," Jamie muttered.

"Hey, I apologised."

"Yeah. Fair enough. So… want to talk about this crisis of yours? Or do you want me to tell you about my plans to ask Helen to move in with me?"

"Move in with you? You've been dating for what… six months?"

"Wow. Two years, Zoe. It's been two years. Mate, sometimes I think you miss how time moves. That is the only reason I can see as to why you've stayed in that shitty job for so long and why you keep putting off dating. Do you know when you last had a girlfriend?"

She glared at her brother. "No, and neither do you."

"Yeah, fair enough but Helen remembers. She said she was worried about you and that you hadn't dated for like three or four years. That's huge, Sis. I mean, you're not ugly and your personality isn't that annoying. You live in Queenswell, which last time I checked was part of Greater London, so there must be loads of lesbians around."

"Woman loving women," she corrected.

Jamie swallowed a sip of latte and stared at her. "Excuse me?"

"It'd be better if you used 'woman loving women' or 'Sapphic women.' I don't just date lesbians, I date bisexual or pansexual women too."

"Zoe. You're not dating anyone at all. That is my point. All you do is moon over celebrities and that middle-aged woman who comes into the bookshop."

"Rebecca Clare isn't middle-aged. She's like in her late thirties or early forties."

"Yeah, and if she lives to be about eighty, that means she is in the middle of her lifetime, aka her age."

Zoe picked up the bag of sweetener again and threw it at her brother. "Oh shut up, you pillock. She's far too hot to be middle-aged."

"Oi, judgemental much? Middle-aged people can be hot too. Hell, old people can be. Look at Helen Mirren."

"Are you trying to tell me that you want me to date Helen Mirren? Because I'm game if she is."

He rolled his eyes. "I'm saying that you can't just sit here and brood about how your life ran away while you were unpacking books. You need to get your arse out there and look for new people and opportunities."

Zoe sighed. "Fine. I'm going to actively go to the library and look for reading opportunities. Say hi to Helen from me and good luck with the moving-in thing. Just warn her that you never do the dishes, all right?"

With that, she got up, leaned down to kiss her brother's short-cropped hair, and walked out before he could lecture her anymore.

***

The library was surprisingly busy as a bunch of kids had escaped from the children's section and were now playing tag in the non-fiction section.

Zoe quickly ducked out of their way and hurried over to where the fiction was kept. It was darker than usual around the book-packed oak shelves. Zoe wondered if the council was saving on electricity. She didn't care. What mattered was that it was quiet in this part of the library and she was surrounded by books that were all free and all hers for the picking.

She got out a crumpled list from her jacket pocket. She always kept a list where she wrote down titles she saw in the bookshop and wanted to read, then she raided the library for them. The newer titles had usually been snapped up but sometimes she got lucky.

As she browsed for C. Robert Cargill, she smelled a familiar scent. She realised it was perfume and at first just ignored it, assuming she had just smelled it on a customer at some point. The scent got stronger as she walked further and when she reached the end of the Cs, she had stopped looking for Cargill and was now concentrating on breathing in the alluring smell. It was a peculiar; sharp like elderberry but tinged with something warmer like vanilla. Zoe wasn't sure, since she had stuck to fruity body sprays ever since she was a teenager. The world of complicated, and probably expensive, perfumes was all strange territory to her.

Soon she realised that she had smelled this heavy perfume before but it had been mixed with something else. Something almost unpleasant but quite normal, something like… rain. She had smelled that perfume mixed with the scent of rain-soaked hair and clothes.

She thought back and added up the facts. It was a female perfume, on a person who was rained on, and, if she was honest, there was only one person she could imagine herself being alert enough around to pick up on their perfume choice; Rebecca Clare.

Zoe froze. Surely this was just a coincidence. It couldn't be her. Zoe couldn't have managed to run into a client she knew from a Central London bookshop out here in leafy Queenswell?

She sniffed the air to try to determine where the woman in question could be. Her nose led her down the row of shelves and she guessed that the scent was coming from the other side of the bookcases. She backed up, looked around the corner, and was rewarded by the sight of Rebecca Clare crouching on the ground picking out a book from the lower shelf.

There were so many ways Zoe could have handled this situation. She could have snuck away and avoided any weirdness. Or she could have walked past, faking not having seen Rebecca, to just accidentally bump into her and get to have a conversation. Or just said, "hi." like a normal person.

What Zoe Achidi did was stare for a long time while the shock made her bag slip slowly from her fingers. It was a largish messenger bag and filled to the brim with stuff that had seemed so essential, but now only made it incredibly heavy and noisy as it landed on the floor. The thud echoed through the quiet library, loud enough to wake the dead.

CHAPTER THREE

Zoe

For a long time, Rebecca just looked at her in puzzlement. The light from a window above glinted off her long plait of copper-coloured hair. She stood up to her impressive full height, aided by the ever-present heels, this time tall boots. She looked at Zoe with a frown.

Zoe felt her stomach clench. Her mind felt hazy, like it was trying to escape the embarrassing situation and dive into unconsciousness. Or maybe escape her body completely.

She took a deep breath. Nothing to worry about, she doesn't know that you were sniffing her out and staring at her, or that you have had a crush on her for weeks. Just act casual and it will all be fine. Just say something. Anything.

"They always hide the best books at the bottom, don't they?" Zoe blurted out. Her voice sounded squeaky. The statement was nonsense as the books were obviously arranged alphabetically. She wanted to scream at herself.

Rebecca laughed. "How nefarious of them. They are clearly trying to mess with my knees by making me crouch down. Sorry, I didn't recognise you at first. You're the girl who works at Darren's Book Nook, aren't you?"

Zoe winced at hearing the object of her daydreams, and in all honesty, a few wet dreams, describing her as a 'girl'.

She saw that Rebecca had noticed the wince and luckily her brain supplied her with a not-so-nonsensical cover this time.

"Sorry about the grimace. I just hate the name of that place. It feels like a bookshop should have a more dignified name, you know?" Zoe said, with a shrug.

"Mm, I agree, actually. Still, it has a good selection of books and staff that clearly love literature, considering you are in a library on your day off."

Zoe looked down and scratched the back of her neck. "Yeah. I come here to borrow some of the books I see in the shop but can't afford to buy. What about you? I've never seen you in Queenswell before, do you live around here too?"

"No, actually. Although it is a nice place." Rebecca looked around, as if the library was the town itself. "I live in a flat in Marylebone."

Zoe frowned in confusion. "And there's no library around there? It's Central London, you must have loads of libraries to choose from."

Rebecca smiled at her and Zoe didn't know how to interpret the gesture. She couldn't decide if she should feel dumb for asking that question or just bask in the pretty smile which carved laugh lines in the perfect mask of Rebecca's makeup.

"My company is considering merging with a smaller recruitment company here in Queenswell and I'm having a meeting with them hideously early tomorrow. So, I thought I'd do a reconnaissance trip today and scope out where their offices were. On the way back to the station I got a little waylaid and ended up outside the library. It was an inviting building so I couldn't help walking in," Rebecca explained.

"Oh, so you weren't looking for reading material?"

"No, not really. I'm quite busy with the book I bought from you the other day, and a few dusty old classics I have promised myself I will catch up on."

"Trying to force yourself through Moby Dick, huh?" Fidgeting, Zoe tucked a few stray curls behind her ear but, as always, the thick hair refused to stay put.

"Finnegan's Wake, actually," Rebecca replied with a frown.

"Whoa. Good luck with that; I gave up after about ten pages."

"So then you know why I keep coming to the shop and buying thrillers instead."

Zoe made another attempt at confining her rebellious curls. "Yep."

There was silence for a moment and Zoe thought desperately of something to say to break it before it had time to settle. But nothing came to her. Nothing that would sound sensible, at least. The seconds ticked on.

Rebecca cleared her throat. "Well, I suppose I should be going. My reconnaissance trip has achieved its purpose and I can't spend all my Sunday browsing a library when my reading list is already full. It was nice meeting you again. I'm sure I'll see you in the shop when I need another thriller to keep me away from Finnegan's Wake."

"Um, yes. Great! I'll see you then."

Rebecca smiled and walked away.

As she watched her go, Zoe's brain supplied her with a flood of things to say. Things like "Mind if I ask what your job is like?" or "Will you be visiting this other recruitment company here in Queenswell often?" or even just a "Good luck with your meeting tomorrow." But the automatic door closed behind Rebecca and Zoe was left there, her bag still sunk to the floor and her heart sinking even deeper than that.

CHAPTER FOUR

Zoe

With a cheese sandwich in one hand and her phone in the other, Zoe flopped down on the sofa. She was calling Helen, but she wasn't picking up.

As the phone's high-pitched beeps continued assaulting her ear, Zoe muttered, "Come on. Pick up. Please tell me you're not busy kissing my brother or something even more gross. Pick up!"

As if she had heard her, Helen finally answered.

"Hey trouble. How are you?"

"Miserable."

"Shocking," Helen drawled.

Zoe tried to stop her involuntary chuckle at the comeback but failed.

"Hey, be nice. I just made a complete arse of myself in front of bloody Rebecca Clare."

"What? How? You're not working today. Wait… you didn't stalk her or anything, did you?"

Zoe wasn't sure just how offended she should be by that.

"No! Um, well, no. Not really. I mean I did sniff her out and stare at her until she caught me."

"You what?"

"It's not as bad as it sounds. She was in the library when I was there and I smelled her perfume. I followed it and there she was, crouched on the floor. Her hair was in her usual plait, and she was wearing that posh coat she's usually got on, but she was wearing jeans underneath it. Jeans, Helen."

Even Zoe could hear how her voice had taken on a dreamy quality when talking about Rebecca.

"Uh, yeah, it's a miracle. 'Woman wears jeans in library'— I can see the headlines of tomorrow's paper now," Helen muttered.

"Oh, come on. I've never seen her in casual clothes. She comes into the shop after work or on her lunch hour, so she's always in her work clothes. Which are always really sexy because they're suits and smart dresses and stuff like that. But today she was wearing jeans and boots."

She heard a whoosh on the line as Helen clearly blew out a long breath.

"Right, okay. Can we get back to the part where you stared at her and 'made an arse of yourself' at any point?"

Zoe sighed. "Do we have to? I just want to eat my sandwich."

"No, no, no. You called me to vent, so spill."

"Fine. When I found her, and looked at her, I kind of didn't know what to say so I just stared at her for ages and then my bag fell. It had hairspray, books, and a water bottle in it so it made this huge bang and scared her and then she stared at me and… well, you get the picture."

"Okay, yes. That sounds bad. It also sounds like something from a sitcom."

Zoe groaned. "I know. She makes me feel like a teenager. Like a freaking schoolgirl with a crush on the teacher. It's pathetic."

"Well then, maybe it's time to act your age and just talk to the woman?"

"I did talk to her a little bit. I mean, it was mainly drivel but I did find out why she was there and where she lives. And that she's not a fan of reading the classics."

"There you go. That's progress."

"Yeah, I suppose," Zoe said before taking a small bite of her sandwich.

"So?"

Zoe swallowed her bite quickly. "What?"

"So, are you going to talk to her more? Maybe ask her out?"

"Ask her out?"

"Yes. You're both adults and able to communicate with each other. Unless you have a reason to think she might be a homophobe and freak out if you ask her, I don't see any reason to not take the chance."

"We've been over this, Helen. Even if she's single, she's not interested in me. She's older, educated, and probably straight."

"Or she might fancy the pants off you but think you are not interested in her because you are younger, less stuffy, and straight as an arrow?"

"But I'm gay."

Helen groaned. "I know that, you moron! I'm saying that maybe she doesn't?"

Zoe took another bite of her sandwich and mumbled, "I'm scared."

"Don't talk with food in your mouth, it's disgusting."

"Sorry, Mummy," Zoe said, rolling her eyes.

"Anyway, yes. I know you're scared. But I think you're scared of more than just losing the chance to ogle a businesswoman that comes into your workplace occasionally. I think you're scared of change."

"Whoa, don't pull any punches, there."

"Look, I love you, but both me and Jamie have tried to sugar coat this message for weeks now. Jamie said that you told him you were 'sick of being you' and that you were unhappy when you had coffee together this morning."

Zoe tried hard not to let her tone sound like a petulant teenager when she replied, "Yeah. What about it?"

"Well, then you know, don't you? It's time for a change. If you won't start with your job, then start with your love life. It's been years since you were in a serious relationship and maybe this is your chance? God knows you're keen enough."

"Ugh. Stop being such a flippin' know it all," Zoe said, adding a groan for effect.

"Okay, you're clearly not listening to me and you keep chewing in my ear so I'm hanging up. Just think about it, Zoe. Can your mushy brain give that a go?"

"I'll ask it for you."

"Cheers. Eat your food and try to stay out of trouble tonight. I'll talk to you soon," Helen said.

"Yeah. Talk soon." Zoe paused. "And, um, thanks. I do really appreciate you listening to me waffling on and wanting to help, even if it might not seem like it."

"I know. You're welcome. Have a good night, Zoe."

"Uh-huh, sure. Bye."

CHAPTER FIVE

Zoe

Zoe rolled her shoulders to keep them from tensing up. Having to deal with tricky customers, like the nine-year-old in front of her right now, always gave her the worst muscle knots.

The young girl looked up at her mother with rage imprinted on her little face.

"Mummy. I don't want more books. I want an iPad. Then I can read books on that."

"Yes, dear. But I doubt that's all you'd do with it. I'd find you trying to hack into my Facebook account again. Or spending your evenings watching kitten videos on YouTube or chatting with your friends," the girl's mother retorted.

This was the third rendition of this quarrel Zoe had to listen to in the twenty minutes they had been in the shop. The arguments from either side hadn't changed, but Zoe's polite smile was slowly changing into a frown.

The mother turned to Zoe.

"Help me out here. There must be some books that will change her mind and keep her occupied?"

"Sure. We don't have a huge children's section but we have a few choices for her age group. Some cute, some funny, and a few really exciting ones," Zoe replied. She turned to the girl. "Would you like to go have a look?"

"No. I have to read in school. I don't want to have to do it when I'm at home."

"What if we found you a totally cool book?"

The girl still looked unimpressed so Zoe changed tactic.

"And you know what? Maybe if you spend some time reading, your mum might let you chat with your friends a little afterwards? Then everyone would be happy, right?"

Zoe hated having to say that, to hint that reading was a chore that needed to be dealt with so that you could have your reward. But she wanted these customers happy and on their way as a queue was forming by the till.

She wished she had a magic wand that she could wave and show the girl how much reading could improve and change your life. How it would let you live so many lives; become an explorer in the 1930s one day and a captain of a space ship the next. She wanted to show the girl how reading would exercise her mind and grow her empathy as she put herself in the shoes of the characters. How she would connect differently with each character when she read their thoughts, compared to in the movies where she would mainly see their actions.

But she could see that the girl had made up her mind. Her mother's insistence, in combination with her connecting books with school and her own stubbornness, meant that she wasn't about to give reading a chance. Zoe could only hope she'd change her mind one day.

"No," the girl screamed. She stuck her lower lip out and crossed her arms over her chest. Zoe didn't have to have kids to know what that meant. No go.

The mother sighed. "Don't shout at the nice lady, sweetheart. If you're rude you don't get dessert tonight, remember?"

Darren came out of the breakroom and headed straight for them. Zoe assumed he had heard the girl's screaming.

"What is all the noise about?" he barked.

Zoe closed her eyes. Darren had the tact of a rhino with ski boots on.

The girl's mother explained the issue they were having with an apologetic smile.

Darren crouched down next to the girl. "Too good for books, huh? Why don't you go buy one of those overpriced videogames to play then and leave us people who actually READ to it?"

He stood up and looked at the mother, who was watching him with a face set in shocked confusion.

"Take your noisy brat and go. As you can see, this shop has people who are going to buy a book in it and I pay this doormat of an employee to serve them, not to bow and curtsy to people who probably can't even bloody read."

The mother gasped and took her daughter by the hand. As she hurried to the door she shouted over her shoulder, "don't expect me to ever set foot in this shop again, and rest assured that I will be telling everybody how I was treated here today."

Darren scoffed and headed back to the office. As he turned, Zoe saw an imprint on his cheek and recognised it as the button on his shirt sleeve. He must have been sleeping in there and using his arm as a pillow.

She knew he had done that before, mainly because she had caught him. Twice. On both occasions, he said that he was just thinking about stocking some new and more unusual genres. Yeah, right. Like he even knew or cared what genres they had.

She sighed. Darren being asleep and being woken up by the scream explained his foul mood. The worst part was that Zoe wasn't surprised at the outburst or the complete lack of professionalism. It was all classic Darren.

He banged the door to the breakroom shut. As Zoe rushed to the till to serve customers, she wondered for the umpteenth time why the hell was she still working for him.

CHAPTER SIX

Zoe

It was a Thursday evening and the shop was ten minutes from closing. Zoe stretched, wishing she had drunk more coffee during the afternoon to keep herself from feeling so sluggish now.

She blew some dust off the top of the till. She should go get a duster to do it properly, but as she was alone in the shop, she preferred not to wander off and leave the place looking unstaffed. Darren had to go out for a meeting, he had said. Zoe suspected he was off to watch greyhound racing or at home reading his beloved Westerns.

The bell above the door chimed. Zoe looked up to give the customer her warmest smile, not showing that she was hoping they would be quick as she was about to start closing up. Her heart skipped a beat. The person at the door was Rebecca Clare.

"Hello there. I know you are about to close, but can I quickly buy a pen?"

"O-of course," Zoe replied.

"Great. My favourite pen betrayed me by leaking just before I left work so I thought I'd indulge in a new one. You sell pens, right?"

Zoe's mind was racing. Yes, they had some pens. But so did the stationery shop that Rebecca must have passed to get here. Had she missed that shop? Or was she just that loyal to Darren's Book Nook?

Zoe pointed to a stand with pens and notebooks next to the till. "Um, yeah. We have a few. Nothing fancy, though."

"That's all right. I don't need fancy, I need something new, reliable, and available," Rebecca replied with what looked like a… smirk?

Zoe swallowed loudly. She was desperately trying to think of something to say.

"That's me. I mean, that's us. Or, you know, that's our pens."

Rebecca gave her a quick glance and Zoe wondered if she was trying to keep from laughing. True to her word, Rebecca was quick in picking out a pen. She chose one of their priciest ones with black ink and handed it to Zoe.

Zoe couldn't help herself. As she reached out to take the pen to run it through the till, she let her fingers brush Rebecca's. Her fingers were cold as she had just come in from the autumn evening but felt soft. Zoe decided that the precious touch was worth the embarrassment and having to pretend like nothing had happened.

With her heart beating like a crazed drumbeat, Zoe took the payment and asked if Rebecca wanted a bag.

"No, that's fine. I'll put it in my handbag. I'll need it at work first thing tomorrow morning."

Zoe's brain quickly switched from thinking about the touch of those fingers to a sudden memory.

"Oh, um, speaking of early mornings. How was your meeting in Queenswell last week?"

She was so proud that she had remembered, and that her speech centre had allowed her to actually formulate a question this time.

"It was… fruitful. It looks like the merger will be going ahead and, considering their company is new but rapidly growing into a booming venture, it will be a bit of a triumph for us. My department head was ecstatic, so it looks good for the Christmas bonus for me and my team."

"Oh cool. Congratulations."

"Thank you. It means I'll be spending more time in Queenswell, so I suppose I might run into you."

Zoe was rarely up the end of town where the library and this other recruitment company, was. She could change that, though. The library was lovely and, if it came with a chance of seeing Rebecca, she'd gladly spend every evening there. She was usually reading or binge-watching TV series on her laptop in the evenings anyway, so why not do that there?

"Um, yeah, I'm in the library in the evenings sometimes, so if you ever pop in there, I'll probably be in the reference room with my laptop or a book. Just, you know, don't scare me to death if I'm wearing headphones."

Rebecca laughed. Zoe was stunned that she had just made Rebecca laugh. And it hadn't even been meant as a joke. What a stroke of luck!

Rebecca put the pen and receipt in her bag and adjusted her glasses. "I'll keep that in mind. Right, I better get to the tube before it gets too late."

"Good luck. Hopefully most of rush hour will be over on your line."

Rebecca sighed. "Hardly. But it's not going to get any calmer for an hour, so I might as well soldier on. I'll see you around… sorry, what is your name?"

"Z-Zoe. It's Zoe."

"Perhaps I will see you in Queenswell then, Zoe. Take care."

"Yeah. Will do. Safe travels."

Rebecca smiled and gave a brief wave as she walked out the door.

Zoe took a deep breath. She had just had a reasonable conversation with Rebecca Clare. And now, Rebecca knew her name and where to find her. All Zoe had to figure out now was if Rebecca had been flirting with her or if she had simply been polite, although she was pretty sure it was option number two. Sadly. She wasn't sure why on earth Rebecca had come all the way over here to get a pen, though. She needed to talk this over. She bit her lip and tried to decide: Helen or Jamie.

***

She knocked on the door and her brother opened, hair wet and clothes thrown on haphazardly.

Zoe frowned. "Oh god, please tell me I didn't interrupt something."

"Would you stop being so paranoid and grossed out about me and Helen? We're all adults, get over it."

He stood aside to let her into the flat before continuing, "And no, I just showered after having lifted some weights. Needed the stress relief after the day I've had."

Jamie worked for the council and Zoe knew it took a toll on him on bad days. Suddenly, she felt guilty about bringing her infatuation-problems to his door.

"Right, um, do you need some alone time to decompress? I can come back."

"Nah, the company will do me good. Bring your bony arse in here."

With a grunt at the comment about her behind, she was quite curvy and proud of it actually, she walked past him into the flat. She went right into the small lounge and sat down on the sofa. He sauntered after her, buttoning his shirt properly and buckling his belt.

"So, what's up?"

Zoe steeled herself. "Don't laugh or think this is ridiculous, but I need to talk about it."

"You're my little sister, everything you say is ridiculous to me."

"Shut your face and listen. I talked to Helen about the last time I ran into Rebecca Clare so this time it's your turn."

He sat down and groaned.

She scowled at him but didn't dignify his behaviour with a comment. "I'm wondering if Helen might have been right about Rebecca liking me in some way."

"Helen's always right. It's her special talent," Jamie said, his voice soft and sappy.

Zoe grinned. "Yeah, I know. Just wait until you have an argument with her. You won't be so happy about her always being right, then."

Jamie ran a hand over his face. "Zoe, for heaven's sake, I've been with her for two years. I've had arguments with her. I know what she's like."

"I still can't believe it's been that long. You sure you didn't get the date wrong?"

"Yes," he said though gritted teeth.

"Fine, fine. Keep your hair on."

"Could we get to the point before I throw you out?"

Zoe fidgeted in her seat. It felt so absurd now. Her brother had real problems, like stress at work and a serious relationship with arguments. What did she have? A possibly semi-flirty conversation with a customer.

"Maybe I shouldn't bother you with this," she said finally.

"Maybe you should. If there has been any kind of progress on the Rebecca front, I want to know. Lay it on me."

She told him about the brief encounter, making sure not to omit the smirk and the laugh. When she had finished, Jamie hummed and looked up at the ceiling.

"I'm no expert on women. Especially not ones who are into birds."

Zoe had always hated the expression "birds"', it was one step away from the American "chicks" which was even worse in her opinion.

Oblivious of her thought process, Jamie continued. "But yeah, it sounds like she might have come in to see you again. And that she liked talking to you. That's a good start. So, now you take the next step."

"Me? I took the next step. I told her I'd be at the library in the evenings. Next step has to be her going there to find me," she said, almost shrilly.

He looked at her with raised eyebrows and arms crossed over his chest.

"What?" she asked.

"You're twenty-six and at a crossroads in your life. Do you really think you should go to that badly heated, old library every evening and just sit there in the vague hope she might pop in? You have to do more than that."

"Like what?"

"Do you know where she works?"

"Yeah, I called her mobile once to let her know her book had arrived and she replied with her name and the name of the company. Acacia Recruitment. It's in her email address too."

"Well, that's even better. You have her email address and her number. Call her and ask her out."

"I can't do that!"

"Why not?"

"Jamie, she was probably just being friendly. And it would be unprofessional if I use the number I was given for work purposes to stalk her."

"You aren't stalking her. You're asking her out, you numpty."

"I can't do it. Especially not like that."

He was quiet for a while, looking at her. When he spoke again, his voice sounded determined.

"All right. Fine. Just wait until she comes in to the shop or until she finds you in the library then, 'kay?"

That pause and the stare from him worried Zoe. She knew her brother well enough to know that he was keeping something from her. She hoped it was just the fact that he thought she was a coward. He stood up.

"I'm gonna get something to eat. I have some leftover tikka masala in the fridge, want some?"

In a wistful tone, Zoe said yes and sat back to gaze out the window while her brother went to the kitchen. The streets below were milling with people even though rush hour was long gone. She couldn't help but wonder if Rebecca had gotten home okay.

CHAPTER SEVEN

Helen

Helen watched Jamie run his hand over the tightly-cropped curls on his head. She loved watching his hands, they were strong and veined but surprisingly soft. She wished she could smooth the worry lines off his handsome face, though.

"I just don't know what we are going to do about her, Hel. Clearly she's not going to get over this Rebecca person anytime soon."

"You know that isn't the only thing she's hung up on. Zoe's stuck in her own life, too scared of reaching her full potential."

"Yeah, love, I know that." He glared at her as if she had just explained that the earth was round. "But we're unlikely to get her to quit that job or to move to a better flat. Dating seems to be a dead end too. This Rebecca person, though… maybe we can do something about her, and that one change will spark something in Zoe to make her get off her deadbeat arse and sort her life out?"

Helen chewed her lower lip. "I suppose. Talking to her doesn't seem to help though. She's convinced that Rebecca Clare is as straight as an arrow and way out of her league."

"I know. But why? Why? Because she's posh or 'cause she's old?"

Helen playfully smacked his shoulder with the back of her hand.

"Don't be so rude! But in all honesty, probably a little of both of those things. That and the fact that your little sister has the self-esteem of an earthworm. She thinks everyone is out of her league."

"So what do we do?"

Helen looked into Jamie's big brown puppy eyes and couldn't even feign annoyance at the fact that she always had to come up with the plans. He and his sister were worth the effort.

"Well, we could try setting them up somehow? Making sure they are in the same spot at the same time and hope your sister grows a pair of balls, sorry, ovaries, and talks to the woman?"

"Nah, too complicated, and Zoe would just chicken out and stay quiet. You know what? If Zoe won't take steps to figure out if Rebecca might be interested, I guess it's up to you and me to do it for her."

"Jamie. Are you suggesting we march up to a complete stranger and ask if she fancies your sister?"

Jamie wasn't looking at her, his gaze was glued to the ceiling.

"Uh-huh. Something like that. I thought about this yesterday when Zoe came by my flat. She talked about having Rebecca's email address and I wondered if I should just email her and say that my sister wants to take her out for coffee. But then I thought that was a daft idea. I think we should just go see her and see what she's about."

Helen sighed. "This is just you all over. No plan, no thinking–just acting."

"Yeah, well. What's lacking in my sister's life is acting, so I'll give her a push."

"Fine. On one condition."

He frowned, his dense eyebrows almost meeting. "What?"

"You don't let Rebecca know what we're up to. I won't have Zoe embarrassed for life here. We need to gage her interest for Zoe, and try to create chances for them to spend more time together, but do it stealthily."

"Okay, Nancy Drew. How the hell do we do that?"

"I think I might just have an idea."

***

They were standing by the reception desk explaining to a woman in grey glasses, which said Calvin Klein on the side, that they wanted to see Rebecca Clare.

"I see. Do you have an appointment?"

"Uh, no. We know that this is a little unconventional but if you could please tell her that it is about Zoe Achidi, who works in Darren's Book Nook. She'll know what that means."

The receptionist looked at them as if they were children who had wandered in and asked for a meeting with Santa Claus.

"I will ring upstairs and relay your message, but I have to warn you that Ms. Clare is very busy."

"Yes, of course. Thank you," Helen replied. She had wondered if this was a good idea and now she was sure that they wouldn't catch even a glimpse of Rebecca.

Helen hoped she was wrong. If she wasn't, they would have unnecessarily gone through the palaver of googling Acacia Recruitment, finding its address, and then traipsing all the way into the heart of London to end up here. Not to mention that they had both taken time off work for this. And, of course, that they had dragged Zoe's name into this, but it had to be done.

Helen looked around, taking in the slate-grey marble floors and walls. A row of black leather chairs was behind them and a reception desk with two stern women was in front of them. One of those women was the Calvin Klein fan and she was just finishing up her call.

"Ms. Clare will be with you shortly. Please take a seat and help yourselves to lemon water," she said with a smile. It didn't reach her eyes.

Helen eyed the huge glass container of water and lemon slices that stood at the end of the reception desk. It had a little metal tap at the front and a pile of clear plastic cups next to it. Helen watched the bright-yellow lemon slices slowly swirl through the water. They looked out of place, everything else here seemed to be muted greys and stark blacks.

The receptionist wasn't looking at them anymore; she had gone back to her computer screen and was typing rapidly.

Jamie, looking for all the world like a lost little boy, had slunk back to the chairs and was gingerly sitting down.

"That chair won't break, you know," Helen joked.

"No. But I feel like it might toss me out of it. Like an ejector seat or something."

"Don't be silly. Why would it?"

"Uh, because I make a third of what these people make every month. And I'm Black."

Helen shook her head. "The receptionist is Black too, with darker skin than yours, sweetheart."

"Fine, then it'll just eject me because I'm poor."

She rolled her eyes at his exaggeration. "You're hardly poor."

"I am compared to these blokes." He nodded towards a man who walked past in a crisp suit which fit so perfectly it looked like it had been sewn right onto his body.

Helen couldn't help but grin. "I know this is probably the wrong thing to say, but you'd be so hot in one of those fancy suits."

He smiled at her. "Marry me one day and I'll get a tailor-made suit. Until then, you'll have to put up with my M&S work suits."

She reached out and squeezed his arm. "You look damn good in those too. You'd make anything look good."

"You're just trying to sweet-talk me so I'll relax," he muttered.

She beamed at him. "Is it working?"

Jamie never had a chance to answer as a woman with perfect posture and a kind, if somewhat wary, smile appeared at his side.

"Hello? I assume you are my two visitors? Ms. Collins and Mr. Achidi. Am I pronouncing that correctly?"

Helen was about to ask how she had guessed but then realised that they were the only two people waiting in reception.

"Uh, yes you are. This is Jamie Achidi and I'm Helen Collins. Sorry to interrupt your workday, we just have a quick question."

If Rebecca was curious or confused about them, it didn't show. But then Helen was quite sure this was the sort of woman who would have a perfect poker face. Posh, professional and polite.

Helen looked closer, partly to try and see beyond the deliberate body language, and partly to see what it was her best friend saw in this woman. She saw what she would describe as a classically beautiful woman who was approaching middle age but was not there yet. Rebecca looked fit and had great posture. Her face showed a polite and open expression, so the situation clearly wasn't unnerving her. Just as Helen thought that, there was what looked like a quick glance over at the security guard. Or had she imagined that?

"A question about someone who works in my local bookshop, I gather? This is quite unusual and I would normally not have taken this meeting but you piqued my interest. Do you want to go to a meeting room?"

Sensing Jamie's body tensing next to her, Helen decided that a stuffy meeting room in this palace of a building was not advisable.

"No, this will be fine. We know this is unconventional and that you're busy. We can just ask you a quick question here and then let you get back to your day."

Rebecca gave them a polite nod and a smile. "All right. Ask away."

Looking at Jamie, who still looked tense, Helen decided that he was going to be more of a silent partner in all of this and so she forged on.

"Zoe Achidi is Jamie's sister, and my best friend. I think you know her? She works at Darren's Book Nook?"

Helen wasn't sure if it was her imagination or if the polite smile on Rebecca's face just turned a little warmer.

"Yes. I've run into her both in the shop and in her local library, as a matter of fact. I have to confess that you mentioning her name was what made me come down and see two strangers without an appointment."

"Right, sorry again for just showing up and being so mysterious. I'll get right to it. As you must have noticed,

Zoe's an intelligent and hardworking person and she is completely wasted on Darren and his neglected money pit of a shop. She stays there out of loyalty but she needs to move on. Move up, you know?"

Rebecca nodded so Helen continued.

"She spoke about you and what you do for a living and mentioned in passing where you work. So, we thought of you and your expertise in recruitment and the connections you must have, and wondered if perhaps you could help her find a better job, somehow? Or maybe just give her some pointers about the best way of applying for jobs? Any help at all, really. She wouldn't ask for herself. We're trying to, you know, help her out. Realise her true potential and all that. Sorry if this is really cheeky."

Rebecca's smile certainly grew this time. "No, it's quite all right. Hmm. I'd love to help but my work doesn't relate directly to recruitment these days; I'm not a consultant. Although, I might be able to help and point her in the right direction. I know very little about Zoe, so I wouldn't quite know what sort of job she would be suited for. However, I would love to discuss it further with her directly and assist in any way I can."

The answer came right away and there was real enthusiasm in Rebecca's voice. Helen tried to suppress the smile she felt creeping into the corners of her mouth. Rebecca's response seemed overly helpful towards someone who just provided you with books occasionally.

Helen had no gaydar at all, so she wouldn't dare to try to guess if Rebecca was romantically interested in Zoe. But there was some kind of interest, even if it was just friendly. The fact that she had come down to meet them right out of the blue proved that.

"That's great. I'll tell her you are willing to help her and to get in touch with you. Okay if she sends you an email?"

"Yes, that would probably be easiest."

"Brilliant. Right, we should be leaving," Jamie said, almost making Helen jump when he broke his stony silence.

"Yes, he's right. We'll get Zoe to get in touch with you, Ms. Clare. Thanks again," Helen said.

"Please, call me Rebecca. I'll look forward to the email."

Helen and Jamie smiled at her and began to walk away. They both turned as she added, "might I ask why the two of you are going to these lengths to help her find a new job?"

Helen stopped herself from squirming under Rebecca's examining gaze.

"Honestly? She's been stuck in this dead-end job, in her tiny flat, and in her uneventful social life for ages. She's miserable but doesn't feel like she deserves any better. We thought that getting some help from you might be the incentive she needs to get something moving."

Rebecca looked taken aback and Helen wondered if it was because of the mention of Zoe's social life or because they were planning this behind Zoe's back.

"I see. Well, that seems like a shame. For someone with Zoe's charisma to be stuck in a situation she is not happy with, I mean. I'll be glad to help her, if she wants my help."

The message was clear. Rebecca was only going to get involved if Zoe wanted her to. Helen sighed in relief, that was the sort of respect and consideration she wanted from anyone in her best friend's life.

What was also stood out to Helen were the words "for someone with Zoe's charisma." That sounded like more than friendly appreciation to her. But it was hard to tell with someone as polished and proper as Rebecca Clare.

"I'll make sure to tell her that this was all our idea and that you're only willing to help if she wants your assistance. Sound okay?" Helen asked.

"Certainly. Take care and thank you for the visit."

"Thank you. And bye," Jamie replied with a nod.

He put his arm around Helen and they walked out. When they were outside the tall building, he stopped and faced her.

"So?"

"So what?" Helen replied.

"So, do you think she fancies Zoe?"

"I don't know. You are better at reading people than I am."

Jamie ran his hand over his chin. "Yeah. I think she likes her. I'm just not sure if she likes her in the way that wants to get in her knickers."

Helen grimaced. "I really don't think you should be talking about people getting into your little sister's knickers."

He scrunched up his nose. "Helen, eww. Did you have to make it weird?"

Then he marched on towards the tube stop with his gaze somewhere in the distance. Helen walked after him in her own pace, aware that she could never keep up with her shorter legs and knowing he would wait patiently for her no matter how long she took.

She felt proud of herself. This was a way to get things moving in Zoe's life, and to get her to pursue things with Rebecca, if possible.

Now she just had to figure out a way to convince Zoe of that. And to keep herself from being killed the second Zoe found out what she and Jamie had done. The thought made her take a deep breath while getting her Oyster card ready and heading down the steps towards to the tube.

CHAPTER EIGHT

Zoe

Zoe's temples had stopped throbbing. She was slowly but surely cooling down after the fit of rage she'd had when Helen called to say what they had done.

Zoe huffed out a breath. She couldn't believe her oldest friend thought it was acceptable to tell her over the phone like that. Coward.

She had been so furious and shouted about how they had embarrassed her in front of Rebecca and gone over her head like she was a child and not a twenty-six-year-old woman. Then she had hung up.

That had been, she checked her wristwatch, seven minutes ago. She was only now breathing calmly again. She was evaluating the situation. How much damage had been done here? There was a silver lining, of course. Rebecca had agreed to help and said nice things about her. But still, she was mortified. Mortified and... terrified. There was no hiding now. Rebecca was expecting her email.

Sure, she could email and say that it was a misunderstanding and that she was happy with the way things were. But that wouldn't help anyone. It would just be awkward and she'd be throwing away her chance. Even amidst her anger and fear, Zoe knew that.

With a deep breath that caught a little, she sat down by her battered old laptop and opened her email. She wrote in the address that she had memorized and then stared at the blank square where she would have to try to be casual, witty, succinct, and professional—all in one. How the hell was she going to do that?

She wrote a quick thank you, apologized for her brother and best friend bothering her at her place of work, and asked when would be a good time and place for her to meet. She ended it with a polite hope that Rebecca was well and her best regards.

Then she amended it.

Then she amended it again.

And once more.

Then she swore at herself and pushed send before she spent any more time on this one, short message. She sat back in the chair and realised that her hands were shaking.

"Bloody hell, woman, get yourself together," she muttered to herself.

She went to put some tea on and maybe try to find some biscuits at the back of her cupboard, she needed to get her blood sugar up after all that.

Tea and half a pack of Bourbons in hand, she went back to sit in front of her laptop. She figured she could watch a few booktuber videos on YouTube while she got some caffeine and sugar into her system.

To her surprise, there was an email. An email from Rebecca Clare.

Zoe stared at it with her mouth full of unchewed biscuit. She felt a buzzing sensation in her stomach but couldn't tell if it was a thrill or the start of a panic attack.

She opened it and started to read, while finally chewing her biscuit.

Dear Zoe,

Yes, I will be glad to help. My father always said that if you reach higher ground, pull others up along with you. Maybe by helping you, I could be following his advice.

As we both clearly know the way to Queenswell library and there seemed to be a few tables available, perhaps we can meet there? Would Saturday work for you? Say 9am?

Looking forward to hearing from you.

Kind regards,

Rebecca Clare

Zoe looked at the words on her screen. Rebecca wanted to pull her up. Zoe wasn't quite sure what that meant but she was ecstatic and couldn't stop herself from fist-pumping into the air. Despite Helen and Jamie saying that Rebecca had seemed happy to help, Zoe had not quite believed it. A part of her had been sure that Rebecca would find a way to nicely get out of the arrangement.

She hurried to reply.

Dear Rebecca,

That sounds great! Thanks. We'll have to make it after 9.30 though because I think that's when the library opens on Saturdays. Maybe say 10 to be sure?

Best,

Zoe

A reply confirming that ten would be good came in soon afterwards and Zoe felt strangely proud that Rebecca was replying so fast. That could simply mean that Rebecca was bored or that she was the type that replied to all correspondence immediately. The latter seemed more likely. Not that Zoe knew that for sure, as with most of her facts about Rebecca, it was all assumptions and educated guesses.

She was going to remedy that soon, though. Saturday at ten. She hoped with every fibre of her being that she wasn't going to be disappointed. Maybe Rebecca would turn out to be way too dull? Or some kind of right-wing crazypants?

No, she was sure that her view of Rebecca was real. Saints know, she had looked closely enough. Every time Rebecca had come into the shop, it had been as if Zoe's senses had heightened. She could remember what Rebecca had said, if she seemed stressed, and what she was wearing for basically all of the many occasions.

That was when it hit her. What she was wearing… what the hell was she going to wear to meet up with Rebecca Clare? To talk about jobs and applications, no less. It had to seem professional, as if she took this seriously, but still be casual enough to make it seem like she hadn't spent days agonizing about what to wear.

Zoe looked over at her small wardrobe and groaned out loud.

CHAPTER NINE

Zoe

The wind was chilly that Saturday morning and Zoe was glad she had put on the posh-looking leather jacket over her knitted cardigan. The jacket was loaned to her by Helen, who had been over the moon to hear that Zoe was seeing Rebecca so soon, and had gladly helped her pick out some clothes.

Helen had focused on making Zoe look business-like and ready to give this opportunity her all, while Zoe had been more worried about looking like she was trying too hard and wondering what the outfit did for her figure. In the end, they had come up with an outfit that looked professional to Helen and casual and attractive enough for Zoe. Black leather jacket, a tight green cardigan, an ironed white shirt, simple boots, and black corduroy trousers.

It all kept the chill out nicely, something Zoe was grateful for now as the late autumn winds were threatening to freeze her bum off.

In her hands were two small takeaway cups. Zoe was worrying that the contents of the cups might grow cold if Rebecca didn't show soon, so she was relieved when she saw her striding her way. She was, as always, a vision. Wearing an elegant charcoal-grey coat, which set off the red in her hair, what looked like skinny black jeans, and long boots. And to top it off, a dazzling smile which made subtle lines appear next to her eyes.

Zoe felt the strange urge to run. Rebecca was too attractive and no borrowed clothes could make her worthy of being in the same room as this woman. Instead of taking off for the hills, she managed to speak.

"Hi. I got us some espressos. I don't know if we're allowed to have drinks in there but I didn't want us to go without caffeine."

Rebecca looked at the two small cups which steamed in the cold air.

"Oh, how thoughtful of you. Espresso is actually my poison of choice so you just made me a very happy woman."

She took one of the cups, sipped it, and, apparently finding it an acceptable temperature, downed the contents in one go.

Zoe looked at her for an awkward amount of time and then followed suit. While the cold air had chilled the espresso, it was still quite hot and Zoe found herself coughing.

"Wow, that was hotter than you made it look. Yeah, you must be used to drinking these," Zoe spluttered.

Rebecca laughed. "Sorry, I've probably got asbestos lining in my throat after having to down one or two of those in a hurry before a presentation or meeting. Are you all right?"

Zoe gave one last cough. "Yeah, I'm fine. Wanna go in?"

Rebecca nodded and walked ahead up the stairs to the entrance. It was only then that Zoe noticed that she was carrying a briefcase, which bulged like it had been overfilled.

She was happy that she had brought a notebook, some pens, and a basic account of her school period and the years she had worked at Darren's.

They sat down at the end of the long table in the library's reference room and Zoe looked around. Tall shelves filled with reference books, most of them old and nicely bound, covered the walls. Some shelves seemed to have broken free and shot off in rows into the room, leaving only enough room for one rectangular table where people could sit. There were a few old men sitting around and reading the newspapers but, other than that, the room was unusually empty. It was clearly not exam time as then the room was always stuffed with students.

She saw Rebecca open her briefcase and bring out a small MacBook. Then she produced a black leather notebook, the pen she had bought in the shop the other day, and a folded newspaper.

"Right. First off, I'm afraid I cannot use Acacia Recruitment to help you. The company specialises in medical staffing and my role has nothing to do with the actual recruitment process these days. However, I'm still able to help you with the fundamentals of job hunting."

"Sure, that makes sense. I just want your insight into how all of this works and, you know, a place to start."

"Good. That I can do. I brought the newspaper if you wanted to look at the job ads in it, but to be frank with you, I think you'd be better off looking online. But we should probably start with looking over your CV; there's no point in looking for jobs unless you have something to send to people."

Zoe nodded, too busy looking at Rebecca's face to find words to reply with. During their brief conversation, her expression had changed from serene pleasantness to business focused. That presence, which Zoe had always loved was now in full force; Rebecca Clare looked like a woman you didn't want to mess with and Zoe felt herself go weak at the knees.

"Perhaps I should start with asking if you already have a CV?" Rebecca said, while tucking the newspaper back into the briefcase.

"Well, no. I wrote down some facts and dates but I don't know exactly what a CV should look like. Sorry."

"Please don't apologize. I have seen some awful CVs and would rather have us create one from scratch than try to fix a bad one. Thank you for coming prepared with all the details and dates."

She looked up at Zoe and gave her a quick smile. It flashed past so rapidly that Zoe almost got whiplash trying to absorb it before it was gone.

"Right, unless you are applying for certain jobs, like government or academic positions where they want you to fill out their specific forms, you will need a CV. And we will make sure you have a strong one."

Rebecca closed her briefcase with a distinct snap and put it to the side. She sat up straighter, popped her knuckles with precise little clicks and locked eyes with Zoe.

"Your friend Helen intimated that you had been at Darren's Book Nook for quite a while?"

"Uh, yeah. Since I was eighteen, actually. My parents kicked me out when I was seventeen and my life broke down. I stayed in my brother's flat until my savings ran out, then I got the job at Darren's a few days after my 18th birthday," Zoe replied before she had time to scold herself for oversharing.

Rebecca made a face that Zoe couldn't interpret.

Ending the rapidly growing silence, Rebecca said, "I'm sorry to hear that. I can't imagine any good reason for parents to throw their children out."

Zoe felt that familiar feeling, the one that everyone who had to come out of the closet got when they had to tell a new person that they were anything other than heterosexual and cis-gendered. That feeling, which had been a strong dread at the start of her out-of-closet life and now had simmered down to a pang of uncertainty. You never knew how people would react or how they would treat you from then on.

Today, that feeling was worse than normally. This was Rebecca Clare. The woman that Zoe wanted so desperately to get to know and keep in her life. Should she change the topic or just wave away the indirect invitation to tell all? Would that seem like she had something to hide? Or seem rude?

Realising that she had been quiet for too long and had to say something, Zoe decided to take the plunge and be honest.

"My mum is from Ireland and my dad is from Cameroon, both strict Catholics. That meant that they weren't too happy about me coming-out as a lesbian. My brother, Jamie, who you met, stood by me and they never forgave him for that. But they at least talk to him, which is more than they do with me."

Zoe cleared her throat. "But never mind that. The best revenge is living well, right? A new job would do that reeeeeally nicely."

Rebecca looked stunned, then furious. But she quickly got her features in order.

"Of course. I gather that this is a painful subject so we'll leave it there. I just have to say that parents, no matter what their beliefs are, should never abandon their child, and I'm terribly sorry that it happened to you. As you say, we will focus on fixing the part of your life that we can fix – your career."

Zoe was happy that Rebecca had understood the hint of warning in her voice and moved on to safer topics, but she couldn't help wonder if it would have been smarter to keep Rebecca talking to see what her views on LGBTQIA+ people were, and more importantly, if she might be one of them. But they were back to business now, as it should be.

Rebecca booted up her MacBook and brought up some CV templates. Zoe tried to give them her full attention, ignoring the smell of Rebecca's alluring perfume and the memory of the angry, almost protective, glint in Rebecca's eyes as she told her what her parents had done.

CHAPTER TEN

Zoe

A week had passed and now it was Saturday again. Zoe's CV had been finished last week; her school and work experiences were quickly jotted down, polished, and expanded upon as much as possible. Rebecca had also recommended that they include other parts of Zoe's life, suggesting that they brand Zoe's helping the neighbours arrange their Sunday coffee mornings as volunteer work. In short, the CV was as primped and filled out as it could be and looked surprisingly professional to Zoe's eyes.

Now came the question of what to do with it.

Now was the time to start looking at what jobs were around.

Now, it was all starting to feel horribly real that Zoe was leaving her old job and getting a new one.

Technically, it had been Zoe's shift at the bookshop this weekend but when she had offered to do some of the crappier jobs throughout the week, Darren had quickly agreed to switch.

Thinking about Darren made Zoe come up with a question. She lowered her voice, not wanting to disturb the old men reading their newspapers and the middle-aged woman who was reading a magazine in, what looked to Zoe, one of the Asian languages.

"When should I tell Darren I'm leaving? Should I tell him I'm looking for work?"

Rebecca seemed to think about that for an inordinate amount of time.

"That depends on your relationship with him. If you know he wants the best for you both, then tell him and he has time to look for a replacement and can support you in your search. If you think he'll take your leaving badly and be vindictive, then you might want to wait until you are ready to hand in your notice," she replied in an equally hushed voice.

Zoe chewed her lip. "He does get really livid when a supplier snubs him or a customer he likes leaves. I don't think he's gonna take this news well."

Rebecca held out her hands in a say-no-more gesture. "Then I suggest you wait, but the decision is yours in the end."

"And if he gets fuming because I didn't tell him earlier?"

"Then he is in the wrong. You have no obligation to tell him before your notice period, and he must realise that if he had a better attitude, you might have confided in him," Rebecca stated calmly.

Zoe tried to look nonchalant but clearly her continued worry was all over her face because Rebecca added, "Just remember that this is Britain; it's illegal for him to straight up give you a bad reference. However, most employers know how to phrase neutral statements to send the message about a bad employee to the next employer. Treat him as fairly as you can and give him more warning if you want to.

But don't let him punish you during your last period of work."

Zoe gave a tight nod. Rebecca placed her hand over Zoe's on the table sending Zoe's heart into overdrive.

"Your concern isn't about how he treats you, is it? It's about doing the right thing."

Zoe looked down at the table and fidgeted in her seat. "Yeah, it is. I don't want to be a prick."

Rebecca slowly withdrew her hand and Zoe felt like hers was tingling where it had been touched.

"Then go ahead and tell him," Rebecca said.

Zoe thought about it, letting Darren's angry, red face flash through her mind.

"I will. But later, right now it's all pie in the sky, you know? If I get called for an interview anywhere, I'll tell him."

"That sounds more than fair. Right, should we start looking for jobs, then?"

Rebecca indicated her MacBook. Zoe nodded in response.

"Now, if you aren't too picky about what jobs you want, I suggest we sign you up to a few agencies and they will contact you if they have an employer who needs you. If you want to be a bit pickier, we will start checking the usual websites."

"I think we can go with picky, right now. I'd like to try getting bookstore jobs, if possible. I know they are far and few between but—"

Rebecca held up her left hand, Zoe quickly noted that there was no wedding ring.

"Say no more. You have a job so it's not like you are desperate, you can afford to shop around and wait for something appropriate to pop up. I've asked around and been told that we should check the big chains first, they rarely use agencies and they seem to advertise on their own websites. Independent shops, well, that is a different kettle of fish. But we'll figure it out."

"Okay, I'm fine with the big chains. I've tried an independent shop, after all."

"That's true. Do you want it to be in Queenswell or are you prepared to keep commuting?"

Zoe smiled. "This is Greater London. Everyone commutes, right? I'm always willing to travel; it gives me time to read."

Rebecca returned the smile and Zoe felt a warmth in her suddenly breathless chest. Get a hold of yourself, she berated herself.

Rebecca brought up the website of the biggest chain of bookstores in the UK and drilled it down to branches in Greater London.

Without thinking it through, Zoe leaned in closer to the screen to get a better view. This obviously meant that she could smell Rebecca's complex perfume and feel the warmth radiating off her well-dressed body. Zoe died a little inside. She had to fight not to groan at the stupidity of getting so close to someone she was meant to be platonic with. She was also fighting not to moan at the closeness of this unobtainable goddess.

She clenched her fists and tried to focus only on the screen.

They kept looking, deciding that she was underqualified for all the jobs in the bigger bookstore chains as most of them seemed to be on a managerial level.

"I can't imagine ever being a manager," Zoe said with a grimace.

"Oh, it's not so bad. You grow into it. Some people are natural leaders and others, like me, have to learn to become one."

Zoe looked away from the screen and right at Rebecca's face. The little lines beside her eyes were barely visible when she wasn't smiling and Zoe had the absurd feeling of missing them.

"You mean you weren't always this…" Zoe trailed off, trying to find the words. Obviously in charge? Calmly dominant? Imposing? Bloody smashing?

Rebecca smiled at her and suggested, "Bossy?"

"Confident," Zoe corrected, while letting her cheeky grin match Rebecca's.

Rebecca's smile didn't fade, it just turned playful. "Ah. No, I wasn't always this confident. I went for a senior post when I was in my mid-thirties and I was terrified. I worried about not getting the job but even more than that, I worried about getting it and failing miserably at it."

She paused to tighten the ponytail that her copper hair was confined in today. Zoe wasn't sure it had needed to be tightened and took the gesture as a reflex or stalling technique. She was trying so hard to learn how to read this woman.

Returning her hands to the table, Rebecca continued speaking.

"I have always been able to make people listen to me. Mainly because I naturally seem to exude some form of calm, which others take for confidence. But calling the shots and knowing the full weight of the decisions resting on my shoulders, that took some getting used to. I almost developed an ulcer in the first six months."

"But then it got better?"

"Yes. I knew by then that any mistakes could usually be mopped up and that I wasn't alone, I had colleagues and superiors to assist and advise me when things got thorny. I'm a firm believer in aiming high and then adjusting to the altitude when you get up there, but I know that isn't for everyone."

"No, it really isn't," Zoe said with a faked shudder. It earned her a smile, which spurred Zoe to keep talking.

"So, you just started climbing in the company and never looked back?"

"Actually, I've switched companies three times since then. Each time going for a higher level of position. But yes, it's been solid work and new challenges ever since."

Zoe saw her chance and took it. "Sounds busy. Doesn't your family mind?"

Rebecca looked uncomfortable for a moment and Zoe was sure that she had overstepped and ruined the more personal chat they finally had going.

"I see my parents every Sunday and my sister lives down in Cornwall, so no. They don't really mind."

No partner. There was no mention of a partner. Zoe fought to keep her features neutral and not celebratory. She was so pleased with her detective work that it didn't even occur to her that she could be gifted with more details, but, as Rebecca kept talking, it seemed to be her lucky day.

Rebecca cleared her throat. "It has wreaked havoc with relationships, of course. Usually because men are threatened by me making more money than them and often women want to settle down and have children. The latter has never been at the top of my priority list."

Zoe felt like time just stopped. Screw that, she felt like the whole world had just stopped. Rebecca Clare had just dropped the bomb that she had been in relationships with women. Zoe hoped that her exterior was calm and unaffected because inside, she had strobing lights, a disco ball, and Celebration by Kool and the Gang playing loud.

"Oh," Zoe managed to croak out.

"Enough about me. I've just thought of a big chain of bookshops. I forgot about them because I think of them as mainly doing stationery. But they sell books, so let's check their website," Rebecca stated.

There could be no arguing with her tone of voice.

Zoe nodded, trying to quiet Kool and the Gang and focus. It took her almost ten minutes of being dazed and happy, and wondering if she should sneak away and tell Helen, before Zoe was back in the room and engaged in checking out the website on the screen. She even managed to sound normal when she agreed that the IT specialist they needed for the Richmond office was not for her.

Rebecca's phone buzzed and drew angry looks from the others in the library's reference room. A man holding a giant book, which seemed to be pictures of birds, even shushed her. Rebecca whispered an apology before leaving the room to take the call outside.

When she was alone, Zoe sneaked out her phone and quickly texted Helen to say,

Holy fudgeballs, Hel! She's bisexual! Or maybe pansexual? Either way, she's into women. Woohoo!

Then she sat back, in such a good mood that she even smiled at the grumpy guy with the bird reference book.

After a few minutes, Rebecca came back.

"Sorry about that. That was a friend asking if I wanted to play squash this afternoon."

Zoe felt a pang of guilt. "Oh. Do you wanna go? I don't want to monopolise your entire Saturday."

"No, she always wins and it's getting tiresome. I'd rather be job hunting, to be honest."

Zoe realised that she was probably not hiding her relief very well. "Okay, cool. So, what's next? Check Gumtree?"

"I wouldn't recommend it. You can find some good jobs on there but I've heard horror stories about dishonest employers and near-slave-labour. We should stick to the normal channels, I think. I feel like I have a responsibility to make sure this is a pleasant experience for you."

"Please don't feel responsible. You are just helping me out. It's my life. I'm the one who got myself into this rut and I'm the one who has to get myself out. You're just showing me where the ladder is. Or something like that."

Rebecca gave a muted little laugh. "So, you are openly admitting that you are stuck in a rut?"

"Uh, yeah." Zoe tapped her fingertips on the table, she hadn't done that since she was in school and about to have a test.

"Sorry, I didn't mean to pry."

"No, you weren't prying. It was a normal question."

"Then may I be bold and ask you why you ended up in that rut? Or would you prefer if we go back to the job search?"

Zoe didn't want the chat to end. She had a chance to get to know Rebecca here, but that meant facing up to some ugly truths.

"I guess... I was scared. I was mediocre in school and then I had my parents tell me that I was a deviant and would end up dying in the gutter before dropping head-first in the fiery pits of hell. I was on my own, sleeping on my brother's sofa. Jamie had just moved away from home and didn't have much money, so he couldn't help me. I had to rely on myself and I felt like I... failed on that front."

"Failed? How so?"

Zoe thought it over, trying to piece the subconscious thoughts and unpleasant reasons into a few neat and sensible sentences.

"I got a job, but just because Darren can't stand it when people cry. And, if I'm honest, because he guessed that I'd do anything to keep the job. I didn't get it because I was good at something. And then I got a flat that's got paper-thin walls and a tiny bathroom. I never tried anything else, because I felt like this was all I could achieve. Why aim for more?"

Rebecca shook her head. "With all due respect, I think you are seeing what happened in the wrong way. Most people, if they were thrown out and traumatized in their teens, would have just curled into a little ball and needed help from the council or the Samaritans. You managed to get yourself a job and a place to live, and quite quickly at that. And let's face it, working in an independent bookstore in London is a dream job for many people. It could have been much worse. You did extremely well, Zoe."

Zoe chewed her lip and then stopped, realising that the gesture might make her look younger. That was the last thing she wanted right now. But the feeling in her chest made her feel very young. Very young and very vulnerable.

Rebecca tilted her head. "Want to go back to the job search?"

"Yes, please," Zoe croaked out.

CHAPTER ELEVEN

Zoe

Saturday finally came around. The week had dragged like treacle. Zoe had been preoccupied at the bookshop, her mind brimming with thoughts of getting a new job and with spending more time with Rebecca.

She couldn't hide from herself that she had become even more fond of Rebecca as they spent more time together. When she looked at Rebecca now, she saw more than the impressive businesswoman who would make her melt into a puddle of swooning goo. She was slowly but surely getting to know Rebecca and she liked what she was finding. There was kindness under the confidence. Zoe had seen traces of that before, but worried it was just politeness. There was also an unexpected sense of humour that only came out by slipping through the cracks of the well-assembled façade.

They were sitting down at their usual spot in the reference room. A tall, gangly man, whom Zoe assumed was a librarian, was going through the reference books opposite them, taking certain books out and putting them on a trolley. Zoe wondered what he was seeing in those books that she wasn't. They all looked like old, hardback reference books to her.

She leaned close to Rebecca and whispered, "What do you think those books have done to be taken away from the others. Can he see from their spines that they are not popular or something?"

She expected Rebecca to make a sensible suggestion, like maybe they looked worn, they were for a display of some kind, or that they needed new labels for their spines. Instead, she looked at the library employee and the books and quite audibly said, "No, those are the books chosen to be taken up into the mothership when he ascends."

Then she went back to unpacking her briefcase and setting up her laptop as if nothing had happened. Had anyone else made the librarian-is-an-alien joke, Zoe wouldn't have batted an eye, but, like all jokes that Rebecca made, it was so unexpected that Zoe broke out in laughter.

Rebecca looked up and gave the slightest hint of a smile. "You've got a lovely laugh."

Zoe tried to look confident, as if she got compliments like that often. "Thanks. And you've got a weird sense of humour."

Rebecca's eyebrows rose and she hurried to explain.

"I—I mean that in a good way. I like your sense of humour. It's... funny."

Zoe had never wanted to bang her head against a table as much as she did just then. Inwardly she groaned to herself. Your sense of humour is funny? What kind of numpty phrases it like that?

The corners of Rebecca's mouth quirked but stopped just shy of a smile.

"I'm glad to hear it. Not everyone gets my jokes, which I why I tend to shy away from making them. Anyway, let's get on with the job search," Rebecca said while taking her glasses out and putting them on.

Zoe wasn't about to let her slip back into work that easily.

"Well, just so you know, I get your jokes, so please make more of them."

"Not sure that's advisable. You laughing seems to have hugely annoyed the man over there," Rebecca said. She gave a subtle nod to the right.

Zoe pretended to be stretching her neck in all directions and when she came to the right she looked at a surly man standing between shelves, holding a thick red tome. He looked like they had insulted his mother.

"Hey, that's the guy with the bird book who got in a right mood when your phone went off last week. I think we're making an enemy."

"Oh good. I haven't had an arch nemesis since I bankrupted and disgraced the last one," Rebecca said matter-of-fact.

For a moment, Zoe hesitated. Rebecca knew how to sound so stern when she wanted to. Then she gathered her wits and laughed at the joke.

Rebecca looked up and winked at her. She actually winked at her. "You really do understand my sense of humour. What a relief."

"Yeah, I'm not sure grumpy git over there, though."

"Perhaps he's got a secret crush on you and resents that I get to spend so much time with you," Rebecca suggested.

Zoe sniggered. "A bit like Darren and you and me, then, huh?"

The words had slipped out before she had thought them through. Not the first time in her life, of course, but still frustrating.

Rebecca cocked her head a little. "Darren has a crush on you? And resents me spending time with you?"

"Um, well, no. The other way around, actually. He has a crush on you and hates that I talk to you when you come into the shop."

Zoe hoped that nothing in what had just been said revealed her own interest in Rebecca. It was bad enough spilling Darren's secret crush; she couldn't make the same mistake with her own.

A hint of a wicked smile played at Rebecca's mouth. "He'd hate the fact that we spend every weekend together, then."

Zoe nearly choked on her own tongue. "Uh, yeah. I'm, uh, still sorry that you have to give up your Saturdays to help me. Whenever you want your squash time back, just say the word. I'm sure I can take it from here."

Rebecca waved the notion away while looking at her laptop. "Don't be absurd. I'll help you right up until the point that you start your new position. It's been years since I had the thrill of the job hunt and I'm enjoying experiencing it vicariously. I like my Saturdays just the way they are."

There was no way Zoe could stop herself from smiling. "Yeah, me too."

Rebecca glanced up. The way her eyes twinkled when she looked up over the rims of her glasses hit Zoe like a punch to the stomach. Or maybe it was because there seemed to be real joy in those eyes. Or maybe even flirtation?

You're imagining things. Things that you want a little too much, Zoe's inner voice chided.

"So, um. What have you got there?" Zoe pointed to the MacBook's screen.

"The websites of some independent bookshops in South London. I thought you could email them. I found these sites after a quick Google search last night. I'm sure there are lots more who just don't have an online presence. If you know of any, or happen to pass one, it might be good to carry a copy of your CV and pop in to see if they are hiring."

"Cool. That makes sense. So, do you want to send me those email addresses you found and I can contact them on my own later."

Rebecca looked almost deflated. It only lasted for a millisecond and then her composed front was back.

"You could do that. I don't mind making up an email template for you to use, though. Perhaps send off a few of the emails together today? Unless you would prefer to do it in private?"

Zoe felt a wholly inappropriate thrill at hearing Rebecca say the words "do it in private" and felt ashamed of her gutter-mind.

"No, no! I'd love for you to help me and to make sure I don't make a tit of myself. I just don't want to waste your free time. Like I said, I already feel bad enough to be taking your Saturdays away and now that I know you googled stuff for me last night too, I feel even worse."

She gave a self-deprecating smile, trying to let that explain her meaning. Rebecca looked like she was thinking something through, but what, Zoe couldn't even begin to guess. She was no closer to being able to read Rebecca.

As she watched Rebecca, she tried to pretend that her eyes weren't seeking out the adorable freckles that were dotted over Rebecca's nose and cheekbones and almost covered by makeup.

"I'm not sure how to make this point without sounding rather pathetic," Rebecca said.

Zoe snorted. "Hey, I'm the one who got so stuck in a rut, that my best friend and brother felt the need to seek out a stranger to ask her to basically pull me out of it. Now that's pathetic."

Rebecca shook her head. "Zoe, I think I told you how little I have in my life at present. There's work, and then seeing my parents on Sundays, then more work, the gym two or three times a week, then more work, the occasional trip to Cornwall to see my sister, or a holiday in the sun and a meaningless twenty-four-hour romance with a stranger. And then more work. Perhaps, you are not the only one unhappy with the state of your life."

"Oh," Zoe replied feebly.

Rebecca looked intensely uncomfortable now, her perfect front was lost.

"Perhaps it's not just you who settled for the only things she felt she could have. Maybe I was bored to tears until your friends came to me and asked me to help you."

There were absolutely no words that Zoe could make herself say. Seeing behind Rebecca's mask was such a rare gift.

The process of getting to know Rebecca had just taken a giant leap. She wasn't perfect and she didn't have it all together. And she was willing to admit that, no matter how embarrassed she looked.

She could feel her daydream crush crumbling. She had fallen for Rebecca's persona and what she assumed her to be. She had put this confident, charming businesswoman on a pedestal, like a perfect statue made of the most exquisite marble. It was only now that she realised how easy it would be to love the red-blooded human in front of her, the woman with flaws and insecurities.

Oh, God. She wanted to kiss her so badly.

"Oh, um, okay. Well, I'm glad I made things less boring. If you need more distraction, I have other parts of my life that need help. I'm rubbish at cleaning for example."

Rebecca laughed. It was a muted, warm laugh and it made Zoe feel strangely comfortable.

"Shhhhh," said grumpy-git man. He had somehow sneaked up on them and appeared at Rebecca's elbow with a scowl and a surprising talent for shushing.

"This is a library. It's for readers. Chatting people have coffee shops," he whispered in a growling tone.

Rebecca looked at him with a wrinkle between her perfectly trimmed eyebrows. "Surely, they are for people who purchase and drink coffee. Hence the name 'coffee shop'?"

He scrunched up his nose at her. "Fine. Chat rooms on the internet, then. They are for chatting."

Rebecca nodded, unperturbed by his rudeness. "Granted. If I and my associate here need to speak online, we will find ourselves a chat room. Now we need to be face to face, so I'm afraid we'll have to make do with this reference room. You'll just have to get references from the books for all three of us, I'm afraid. Terribly sorry about that. We will, however, try to keep the volume of the conversation down."

He looked at her as if she had just spit on his shoes but clearly couldn't come up with a counterargument. He muttered, "plebeians", and walked off back to the shelves of books.

Rebecca looked at Zoe with a quirk of the eyebrow that made her chuckle, she put her hand over her mouth to stifle it but was too late. She saw grumpy git turn and give her a withering look before continuing over to the dictionaries.

"I bet he's gonna go look up 'coffee shops' to see if it mentions chatting or not. If it does, he'll be back here to stick the book under your nose," Zoe whispered.

Rebecca adjusted her rimless glasses. "Oh ignore him. He's just frustrated because all his clothes seem to smell of cabbage. Can't blame him really."

Zoe sniggered again, feeling like a naughty kid making fun of the teacher.

Rebecca looked up at her, matching her smile. "Thank you for laughing at my jokes. It's a tough job but someone has to do it."

"If it's a job then I think I'm the perfect candidate for the position," Zoe said, doing her best impression of what she thought you should sound like in a job interview.

"You've got the position, Ms. Achidi. The pay and the benefits are terrible but the hours are very flexible."

"Sounds like my kinda thing. Do I need a uniform?" Zoe said, her mouth once more bypassing her brain again. She evaluated what she had just said and decided that it could sound platonic if her voice hadn't sounded suggestive in any way.

Rebecca gave a little hum, opened her mouth and then closed it again.

In fascination, Zoe watched the composed front slowly but firmly settle in over Rebecca's features once more.

"No, this particular position doesn't. I suppose the jobs we should be looking for might, at least if you do get a position in one of the bookstore chains. Have you been keeping an eye on their hiring pages?"

And they were back to serious again. Zoe felt almost bereft. It felt like having had a bucket of cold water poured over her head too. She tried to ignore it.

"Yep, in fact, I've been checking them almost every evening. Nothing new so far."

Rebecca gave a quick nod. "I'm glad you are keeping on top of it. You never know when an opening for a shop assistant might come up."

Zoe gave what she hoped was a grateful and agreeing nod. Yep, back to being serious.

CHAPTER TWELVE

Zoe

Zoe wondered why late Tuesday afternoons were always so busy in the bookshop. Was Tuesday somehow the day when everyone felt the tug of a new book? As she considered the ages of the older teenagers milling about, she realised that perhaps it was just a school which let out at about this time. She liked being busy, it made time go by more quickly, but this was a little too much for comfort.

Darren wasn't helping. He was in a manic mood today, the very opposite of his usual lazy self. He had just bought a new car and felt the need to tell every customer about it. That would have been fine if he had been willing to serve them while he did so, but no, that fell to Zoe as usual.

One of the customers, a teenage boy with a wispy little beard, asked to see pictures and Zoe had never seen Darren run to the backroom to get his phone so quickly. As soon as he had run off and left the teenage boy to saunter over to the nearby travel section, the bell above the door chimed again and Zoe turned around, expecting another teenager.

That was why she was even more ecstatic than normal to see Rebecca stride in. The heels of her long, black boots clicked on the floor and Zoe was sure she could hear the rustle of her long coat as she moved. Although, she knew that her mind was probably playing tricks on her. She wondered what was next – seeing Rebecca move in slow motion? Ridiculous.

Rebecca smiled at her. "Hello there, Zoe. How are you?"

"Not bad. It's been busy in here today but that's good news for the cash flow, I guess. You?"

"Fine. My four thirty meeting was cancelled so I came out for some fresh air. I thought I'd pop in and see how you were doing. All alone, I see?"

"Yep," Zoe replied.

She didn't feel like explaining where Darren was; she wasn't going to ruin this wonderful surprise by talking about him. Rebecca was here. To see her. Who cared about Darren? Besides, he never managed to find his phone in his grubby old holdall so he'd be ages yet.

"Good. Then I can tell you about the job I've spotted for you. It's an independent bookshop and you fit their requirements. However, it's a specialty bookshop. How do you feel about subjects like tantric sex, healing crystals, and centaur erotica?"

Zoe tried for her best alarmed face and Rebecca nodded with half a smile.

"Out of your comfort zone. I understand. To be honest, the pay was quite shocking anyway. We'll keep looking. The perfect position will be out there waiting for you. See you on Saturday for more job hunting?"

"I've got the Saturday shift again but I'm sure I can switch with Darren if I bribe him with doing the inventory all by myself next time."

"Excellent. Let me know if you need to reschedule. Right, I should get back to work."

Zoe couldn't stop a huge grin forming. "Okay, well don't work too hard and I'll probably see you on Saturday."

The door to the backroom shut with its usual creak and thud, and Zoe realised that Darren must be coming back.

To warn Rebecca not to talk about jobs, she shouted over her shoulder, "Hey Darren. We've got one of our regulars in today. It's Ms. Clare."

Normally, a statement like that would have made Darren ask why the hell she was telling him, but his crush on Rebecca was as fervent as ever and Zoe heard his steps pick up speed.

"Ah, perfect. Just in time to join this young man in viewing some pictures of my stunning new Mitsubishi. Look at this beauty." He pointed to a picture on his phone and then swiped it away to reveal another one, and another one, and another one.

Rebecca gave a polite, fake smile. "Very nice indeed. Sadly, I'm afraid I need to get going. I just popped in to see if my ordered book had arrived but it seems it hasn't. I will just have to wait until you contact me to let me know. Thank you, Zoe."

"You're very welcome, Ms. Clare."

Zoe's tone was polite but her smile was conspiratorial. She'd be lying if she said she didn't enjoy the secret of their friendship. Or mentoring, or whatever it was.

Rebecca left the shop and Darren and Zoe watched the door close behind her. They both jumped when the teenage boy sidled over to them, having forgotten all about him. In his hand was a travel guide to Thailand. His eyes looked... expectant?

He beamed at Darren and said, "So, will you be looking for someone full-time or part-time?"

Darren frowned. "You wha'?"

The teen pointed at Zoe. "When she leaves?"

Darren looked at Zoe and she felt her stomach turn. Her brain was shouting at her to change the topic and get this annoying kid out of the shop before he ruined everything. But there she stood, frozen to the spot, unsure of what to say.

As Zoe wasn't saying anything, Darren looked back to the barely-bearded teenager. Clearly oblivious to that anything was wrong, the teen kept speaking.

"Yeah. I heard her talking to the redheaded MILF who was just here. Since she's looking for jobs, I assume she's leaving this one and I just started looking for work. I mean I have no idea how it works, you know, getting a job and all that. But my mum says that if I don't bring in a little money to the house, she's gonna stop doing my laundry."

Zoe wanted to get tweezers and pluck his ridiculous excuse of a beard one greasy hair at a time. Or strangle him. Yeah, that would be easier and it would make him shut up.

The panic was finally letting go of its death grip on her throat and she managed to mumble, "I think you've got the wrong end of the stick there."

"Nah, mate. I heard you were looking for work. Can't guess why though, this looks like a pretty cushy job. Just stand there and take money. I could do that. Well, after school that is. When are you leaving?"

He asked Zoe the question as if he had asked if she knew the time. She tried not to hate his guts, he was young and clearly not the sharpest tool in the shed. He had no idea how looking for jobs worked. It hadn't occurred to the annoying kid that you don't just get a job out of the blue and that while you spend ages looking, you don't necessarily tell your employer. The employer who might be standing next to you right now. With his face going red and his grip on his phone showing white knuckles.

"I, um, I'm not... um. I mean, I'm just looking around," Zoe said, wishing she was a better liar.

The teen looked confounded. "Really? Sounded pretty serious to me. If you are seeing that ginger Dragon's Den woman on Saturday to look at jobs."

There was a heartbeat of silence before Darren slammed his phone down on the counter.

"Even if I had a million jobs, you wouldn't be getting any of them, mate. Get out of my shop and go home and ask your mum how to apply for work. She'll open your eyes for ya. Get going," Darren muttered.

He wasn't looking at the kid when he spoke to him, though. His eyes were locked on Zoe. As she saw the teenager saunter out of the shop with a confused look on his face, she felt her heart pound and her palms start to sweat. She hated confrontations like these, they reminded her of her last talk with her parents. She tried not to panic.

As soon as the door closed behind the kid, Darren growled, "Right. Do you want to start explaining what you are doing with Rebecca Clare and why it includes looking for jobs? Or should I just assume the worst?"

It wasn't clear to Zoe if he was most angry about her looking for other jobs or about her having a close relationship with the woman they were both crushing on. In the end, it amounted to the same thing – he was livid.

Zoe wasn't the lying type, nor did she know how to smooth things over. She took a deep breath, steadied her hands on the counter, and faced him.

"She's been helping me see what jobs are around. I was thinking that it might be time for me to move on. I mean, I've been here for almost a decade and I think both you and

I could do with a change? You could get someone in here with more bookshop experience and they might be able to show you how to market or rearrange the shop to make more profit, maybe? And I could get a new challenge."

He crossed his arms over his chest. "Oh, I see. This place isn't challenging enough for ya?"

"There's nothing wrong with the shop. Or you." Maybe she could lie after all? "I just think it's time to try something new."

He looked at her as if she had slapped him and he was considering slapping her back. "Fine. So, I suppose you'll be handing in your notice right now then?" He shook his head and mumbled, "Unreliable little bitch…"

"Darren. I'm sorry I didn't tell you that I was looking around. I was going to tell you when I had found something I might want to apply for. But no matter what, you can't call me that."

"My shop. My fuckin' choice of language. Don't like it, lump it. Oh, yeah, you already are. You just didn't tell me. Like you didn't tell me that you knew that posh bloody Clare woman. Is she your godmother or something?"

"No. She's… a friend." Zoe hesitated, not knowing what her relationship to Rebecca was. Darren interpreted it differently.

"What was that tone? 'Friend?' HA! Are you still under the impression you stand a chance with her? Give over. She's not gonna be… like you. And even if she was, she'd be wanting an adult with something to show for themselves."

Zoe felt her blood grow hotter. "Actually. She is 'like me' if you mean that she's into women. And maybe me leaving this dump means I can be someone with something to show for myself."

"Fine. Run out on me after I saved you and took pity on you. No one else is going to give you a job, you bitch. You have hardly any qualifications and no drive. Do you think that because you're black and gay the world owes you a job? You can't play the pity card with everyone, you know. They'll see that you're useless! You are like a bloody doormat, just lying there and letting people walk over you while you do absolutely nothing of use."

"Yeah? Nothing of use? You'll find out just how true that is when I leave and you have to do everything yourself here. Do you even know how to work the computer system properly? How to do the accounts? Where we are up to in the ordered books? You are the one who is useless around here. You want me to leave right away? Without a notice period or a handover? Great, I will."

"Yeah, you bleedin' well will! No last weeks of milking this place for money for you. I want you out of my sight."

"That can be arranged, you knobhead," Zoe said and stormed to the backroom.

She got her rucksack and coat. Then she strode out, past Darren and through the door, not even bothering to close it after herself. She could feel his glare at her back before she heard him slam the door shut.

She walked down the street, no direction, no idea of what she was going to do. All she had was a chest full of rage and eyes full of unshed tears.

Her mind was trying to interject that what Darren had just suggested couldn't be legal but then she knew that she didn't want to stay in his shop longer than she had to. He had reacted just how she had expected. He always took everything personally and always flew off the handle. She understood his anger. What she couldn't forgive were the things he had called her. No, if she could avoid working her notice period, she would.

She looked up and noticed that she was standing outside the headquarters of Rebecca's company. Had that been deliberate on some subconscious level? She wasn't sure.

She stood staring at the tall building through the haze of the tears lining her eyes. She should call Helen and tell her everything. Or even Jamie, he'd leave work and come pick her up.

Instead, she dried away her tears with her fingers, careful not to wipe away the subtle mascara she always wore to work. She sniffed a few times and straightened her back. And walked in through the automatic doors.

CHAPTER THIRTEEN

Zoe

The woman at the reception desk stared at her. Or maybe she just looked her over and Zoe's emotional state made her see it as worse than it was.

Zoe managed to ask for Rebecca Clare and give her own name. Then she took the proffered lemon water and sat down. She looked down at her feet and sipped at her drink, feeling like a little girl alone in a doctor's waiting room.

She couldn't for the life of her figure out why this had seemed like a good idea. She could be crying over the phone to Helen right now or be waiting for her brother's beat up old MINI to come get her. Instead she was here, waiting for Rebecca, without a clue what to say when she saw her.

She heard the familiar clicking of heels and turned to see Rebecca rush down a set of stairs, tap her identity card on a machine, and then come through a turnstile into the reception area.

Rebecca hurried over to Zoe with a look of concern and crouched down next to her chair. Zoe was impressed that anyone could balance in a crouch like that in those high heels.

"Zoe. Is everything all right? Karen said that I had a rather upset visitor and gave your name. I've known Karen for three years and she has never used the words 'rather upset' or any descriptors at all for visitors, so I assumed the worst."

Zoe felt strangely happy that Rebecca had hurried down and that her rapid rambling showed her concern.

"I'm, um, I'm okay. I just… got fired."

Rebecca's sculpted eyebrows rose. "Fired?"

"Yeah. Or actually, I think I quit. And Darren, the bastard, said some really shitty things. And, and, and… I'm sorry to be here bothering you at work. I just… didn't know where to go."

Rebecca ran her hand over Zoe's upper arm. The touch was light, almost over just as soon as it had begun, but Zoe felt it as if the touch had left a permanent mark.

"Don't worry about that. You just saved me from a very dull lecture from one of the IT guys about how I treat my MacBook. Do you want to come with me into a meeting room? I'd like to know what happened, especially what Darren said to you."

"Um, yeah, sure. If I'm not taking up too much of your time?"

"No, no. It's a slow day and it'll be home time soon anyway. Come with me," Rebecca said.

Zoe rose, a little unsteadily. She put her empty glass of lemon water down on her chair and stumbled after Rebecca. She was talking to the guy in a uniform standing next to the machine she had used her card on. The guy nodded and used a key to open the turnstile completely.

Rebecca indicated the way through with a sweeping gesture of her hand. It came close enough to Zoe for her to see that the hand had little freckles just below the knuckles. She walked through and heard Rebecca's heels behind her.

"Now what?" Zoe croaked.

That hand on her arm was back. It felt warm even through Zoe's shirt, cardigan, and jacket. Or perhaps her senses were playing tricks on her. Rebecca removed her hand and Zoe realised just how much she needed physical comfort. She needed a hug. Why, oh why hadn't she called Helen?

Rebecca pointed forwards. "This way. There is a small meeting room right up those stairs. It's the smallest one in the building so it's usually not booked; we should be able to nab it for a little while."

Rebecca began walking up the stairs that Zoe had seen her hurry down a few minutes before. After a deep, steadying breath, Zoe followed her.

The small room they entered was surprisingly cosy, considering how much of this building seemed to be made of glass and marble. There was a round table in the middle and it was surrounded by four chairs. The window showed a view of the skyscraper next door, sleek and gleaming in the afternoon light. It made Zoe feel intimidated and even more emotional than she already was, so she focused back on the cosy room and Rebecca.

Rebecca walked over to a grey phone mounted on the wall next to the door. She picked it up and dialled.

"Hello Karen? This is Rebecca Clare. We are in meeting room 1A and I forgot to order up some tea and biscuits. Yes, the meeting should be ongoing for at least half an hour so please book it for me and have the refreshments sent up. Thank you, and I apologise for not thinking to book it earlier."

She hung up the phone, pulled out a chair, and sat down. She looked up at Zoe. "We're only allowed tea and biscuits sent up for meetings lasting longer than half an hour. It's a new rule and utterly absurd. But I think you can do with the caffeine and sugar after your day, so we'll have to fake a long meeting."

"Sure. I can pretend to be a particularly difficult supplier of hand soap or something," Zoe said as she sat down opposite Rebecca.

Rebecca laughed and the sound was like a balm to Zoe's nerves.

"The building's soap dispensers are not really my purview, but I'll make an exception for you," Rebecca said with the hint of a smile.

"Glad to hear it," Zoe mumbled. She was starting to feel uncomfortable. *What the hell am I doing here?*

They sat quietly for a few moments until the awkward silence was interrupted by a discreet knock on the door.

Rebecca got up and opened it, letting the woman from reception in. The receptionist was carrying a silver tray which had an industrial-looking canister of hot water, a metal tin, which was opened to display sachets of instant coffee, tea bags and small packets of sugar, and milk on it. There was also a small plate with neat, pale-looking biscuits.

"Thank you, Karen."

"You're welcome, Ms. Clare. The room is booked and I have notified your department that you are in a meeting."

"Excellent. Thank you again."

Karen nodded and left the room, closing the door soundlessly behind her.

Zoe surveyed Rebecca as she took the items off the tray and put them on the table. Perhaps it was her imagination, but Rebecca's impenetrable front was even stronger here in her work place.

Zoe realised with a chill that she couldn't read her at all. The words and gentle touches of the arm showed concern, but it could just be down to good breeding and being a people-person. Zoe hadn't been able to see real, naked emotion since she saw Rebecca hurry down those stairs. Maybe she was making a big deal out of nothing. She just wished that Rebecca would stop seeming so... professional, right now.

"Would you like coffee or tea?"

Zoe was one of those rare Brits who couldn't stand instant coffee so she decided tea was her best bet here. She didn't care anyway, she just wanted something to do with her hands.

"Tea please. And at least half of those pathetic little biscuits."

That hint of a smile was back on Rebecca's lips. "Yes, they're not the pride of Scotland exactly, but they are passable shortbread and will at least raise your blood sugar a bit. When they have done their job, you can tell me what happened, perhaps?"

"Yeah. Sure," Zoe said, before accepting the cup of hot water and tea bag that Rebecca handed her.

The tea was spreading in the hot water, making golden brown swirls in the white cup. The water darkened as Zoe looked down at it, unwilling to face Rebecca.

"Milk or sugar?"

"Milk, please. No sugar."

Rebecca handed her a sealed little plastic tub of milk and Zoe opened it and upended it into her cup. The milk spread into the brown water, making swirls of its own until Zoe ruined the pattern with her plastic spoon.

The room was uncomfortably quiet until Rebecca took off her glasses and put them down on the table and said, "You know, the managing director told me that when he started here they had little, white pots of fresh milk and a silver sugar bowl. Times have changed. Which is why most people go get Starbucks before meetings instead of bothering with these refreshment trays."

Having finished her statement, Rebecca poured herself some water and dissolved the coffee in it. Her movements were as calm and precise as always.

Did she say Starbucks?

Clearly Zoe wasn't the only one in this building who didn't like instant coffee. She watched as Rebecca made her coffee and took a sip, without blowing on the hot liquid. Asbestos lining in the throat, Zoe remembered her saying. She wished they were back in the library now, it would have been easier to talk to Rebecca there.

Zoe picked up one of the neat little shortbread biscuits and plonked the whole thing in her mouth. It tasted better than it looked, but it was still a little too stale for Zoe's liking. She chased it down with some tea.

Rebecca waited for Zoe to swallow, then she put her coffee down and looked at Zoe expectantly.

"So, ready to tell me what happened?"

Zoe took a deep breath and blew it out. Then she gave a quick account of what had happened after Rebecca left Darren's Book Nook. The teenager and his blurting out of the truth, Darren's red face and offensive comments and, finally, how they left it, with Zoe rushing off and agreeing to no notice period.

Zoe had expected the business-minded Rebecca to clamp down on the fact that Zoe was now leaving without a notice period or any extra payments. In fact, Zoe wasn't even sure if she was going to get paid for this month considering it was only the 6th today. She was almost ready for a scolding since she had just shot herself in the foot, financially and career-wise.

What Rebecca said instead took her by surprise.

"He said those things to you? He brought up your ethnicity and sexual orientation?"

"Well, um, yeah. I mean, he kinda just stated the facts about that. To tell me that being a minority wasn't going to get me a job. Which shows how little he knows about being a minority. He definitely called me a bitch twice, though."

Rebecca's jaw set, a muscle twitched just beneath her ear. Then Rebecca breathed in deeply through her nose. Zoe wasn't sure what was going on here.

"Whether they are facts or not doesn't matter, Zoe. Your sexual orientation and ethnicity should be irrelevant to your employer and the fact that he used them against you in an argument is unforgivable. He is breaking so many rules of the workplace. Not to mention the personal attacks on your character and the name calling. You have more than enough material to take him to court. Your union will rip him apart. Was the teenage boy present for this? Could he be a witness?"

Zoe felt confused. This wasn't where she had seen this conversation going and she certainly hadn't expected Rebecca to be sounding like she was spitting venom. She had wanted to see something other than polite and professional courtesy from Rebecca, and she was seeing it now. The woman sitting opposite her was livid.

"Uh, no. The kid had gone by then. And I'm not a part of any union even though I know I should be. Look, I don't want to take him to court. In fact, I don't want to see him again at all," Zoe admitted, her voice trembling in an embarrassing way.

Rebecca was looking at her. There was a line between her eyebrows and a tight set to her mouth. Zoe wondered if she was disappointed. Maybe she expected Zoe to fight and thought she was weak for not standing up for herself.

"I suppose you walking out and leaving him to try to manage the store without you could be seen as punishment enough. But it grates on me to let someone treat... an employee like that without harsher consequences," Rebecca said, her gaze now fixed out the window.

"Look, I don't care about him. I just don't want to see him again for my sake. I'm sorry if that makes me a loser in your eyes."

Rebecca's head snapped back towards Zoe. "A loser? Of course not. When confronted like that and in the middle of a rage attack from someone in a position of power, most people would have crumbled. Even apologized and begged to be kept on. Especially as you feel you owe him so much and he is your first and only boss. You stood your ground and refused to let him verbally abuse you, that shows strength."

Zoe felt her unease lift a little; it was crazy how much Rebecca's approval meant to her. And now she knew why she had wanted to come here instead of going to Helen or Jamie. She wanted Rebecca's confirmation that she had done the right thing. Well, that and she always felt the need to see Rebecca.

Zoe observed her closely. Rebecca's coffee stood abandoned on the table next to her folded-up glasses. The frown lines between her eyes were gone and her mouth had relaxed, but that jaw muscle was still twitching violently.

Suddenly, Rebecca got up and started pacing to the window and back again.

"Right. If you are sure you don't want to take Darren to court, get your lawful notice period and make him pay recompense for his abusive comments, then I suppose you need to move on to the next step in your job hunting. We have to ramp it up."

"We? You don't need to help me. This is not a chilled out search for the perfect job anymore. I just need to get out there and find a pay check asap. I'll probably just apply for a job in a fish-and-chip shop or something," Zoe said.

Rebecca stopped next to where Zoe sat and leaned down so they were at the same eye level. She reached her hand out as if to touch Zoe's face and then retracted it immediately as though she was about to be burned.

"If that is what you want, of course. I do believe you can get a job nearer your sector in a manageable amount of time but, either way, I'd like to help you. I know you feel like you're wasting my time but I thought I had explained that I enjoy spending time with you. I mean, I enjoy helping you."

Zoe met her gaze, her eyes locking with a determined pair of blue-green ones. She watched as the light made the two colours blur into a deep turquoise. Rebecca was so close and she was clearly not going to move until she was sure that Zoe had understood her sincerity. Rebecca's presence was, as always, a magnetic pull and Zoe couldn't look away even if she had wanted to.

She was desperate to know what Rebecca was thinking. It was obvious that Rebecca cared but what were her feelings when it came to the two of them? Did she see Zoe as a pet project, as a friend, as someone to mentor or, even worse, were her feelings somehow maternal?

Suddenly the clock on the wall seemed to be ticking unnaturally loud. It sounded like a countdown. Every tick bringing her closer to what had to happen. To action.

She felt bone-tired from all the emotional turmoil and her panic but there was a manic energy that wouldn't let her relax. A survival instinct or adrenaline rush perhaps. She had gone from the most unnerving confrontation of her life, not counting when her parents threw her out, to rushing straight towards the woman who terrified and thrilled her. She had truly tested her nerves and her heart.

And now here she was. So close to Rebecca. Driving herself crazy with trying to figure out what Rebecca was feeling without having to ask and endanger their fragile new friendship.

The ticking was stressing her out, making her heart race. She couldn't shake the feeling of a countdown. But to what? To running away? To asking Rebecca what her intentions were? To blurt out her own attraction?

Zoe's palms were sweaty. She knew it had only been a handful of seconds since Rebecca had last spoken and they hadn't been locked like this for long. It just felt like it. It felt like the painful rush of her heart and the ticking of that damned clock had been plaguing her for hours.

She couldn't stand it. The whole day had been too much and she knew that she was dangerously close to snapping. She didn't want to start crying in front of Rebecca. Or shouting. Or laughing hysterically.

She wished she was one of those calm, collected people who knew how to control themselves. But she was sensitive and emotional and completely out of her depth in so many ways.

And she couldn't control herself.

And the clock ticked down the seconds.

And if she didn't do something, she would scream.

And she was so lonely and she needed…

Needed…

She made a sound somewhere between a whimper and a sob and pushed her face forwards to connect her lips with Rebecca's. She kissed her again and again, letting her lips meet Rebecca's warm mouth in every way she could. She had no idea what she was doing or if Rebecca was reciprocating. She was all instinct and panic.

And then her brain caught up with her and she realised what she had just done. She moved away from Rebecca, whispered an "I'm so sorry" and got up so fast she knocked her chair to the floor.

She ran out of the room, down the stairs and, when she got to the turnstile, she jumped over it and sprinted out to the street. She ran until the sensible voice in her head ceased screaming at her for ruining all her chances with Rebecca. Until it stopped asking her if that had been some form of sexual assault. Until it stopped saying anything at all.

When she stopped, she was by a set of traffic lights on a major road, in a part of town she didn't recognize and she was drenched in sweat. She also realised that she was crying.

She leaned against the building closest and let herself drop down into a sitting position, hoping that no one would come over and ask if she was okay. She couldn't face strangers right now.

She took out her phone and rang Jamie.

CHAPTER FOURTEEN

Zoe

Zoe still felt dazed, almost numb. She was sitting on Jamie's sofa and watching Helen storm in and take her coat off.

Jamie was in the kitchen making tea, which he had been doing for the last fifteen minutes. Proving that he was hiding and freaking out.

Having hung up her outerwear, Helen sat down next to Zoe.

"Jamie told me everything over the phone. I can't believe Darren did that to you. I feel like going over there and kicking him in the knackers!"

"Never mind him. He's a wanker and I'm better off far away from him. I just need to get a new job. Any job. I don't care what I have to do or what hours I have to work. Right now, I'm more worried about… the Rebecca situation."

Helen scratched her neck. "Well yeah, that is tricky. But I don't think you should downplay the job thingy. You know what the job market is like right now. Finding something won't be easy."

"Helen! Will you let me freak out about one disaster at a time?"

Helen held her hands out in a calming gesture. "Sure, I just wasn't sure that this was the most pressing of your two disasters. But hey, whatever you need, love."

There was nothing Zoe could think to say, words seemed so inadequate. She let herself lean towards Helen on the sofa until her forehead was on Helen's shoulder. Helen put her arms around her and pulled her into a tight hug.

"Hey, it'll be okay. We'll find a way to help you with both the work thing and the Rebecca thing."

Zoe just hummed into Helen's shoulder, not wanting to commit to that sort of confidence. They sat like that for a while and listened to Jamie moving cups around in the kitchen. Zoe knew that he wasn't the kind of bloke that minded talking about emotions or freaked out when seeing people cry; he saw a lot of that while working for the council. She assumed that her current situation was so weird that even he didn't know what to say or do.

She felt Helen giggle and grunted out, "What's so funny?"

"Was she wearing lipstick? When we met her she was wearing this really vibrant maroon lipstick and I'm afraid I've got this image of her standing in a posh meeting room with lipstick smeared and eyes the size of saucers."

"Stop giggling. It wasn't funny. I might have breached the rule of certain consent; you know how important that is. And no, I didn't smear her lipstick. She was wearing some, I think, but the kiss wasn't involved enough to mess up her makeup. I didn't make out with her or anything!"

"Okay, okay, sorry. I was just trying to break the tension. I know how important consent is. Look, for what it's worth… Jamie said that she told you she wanted to spend time with you. That in combination with all the subtle flirting and all the hints she's been dropping, I think she's into you. So, it's really likely that she wanted to be kissed."

"But 'likely' isn't good enough, Helen. If we're wrong – I attacked her."

"The whole situation is a bit of a mess. But the kiss was a weird panic reaction and not some predator move. Just call her and explain that."

Zoe groaned into Helen's sweater-clad shoulder. "No way. I can't imagine she would ever want to hear from me again. I'm going to leave her alone."

She heard Jamie's footsteps coming in from the kitchen and felt Helen's head raise. She knew that they must be making eye contact over her head but was not sure what that was conveying. Pity? Confusion? Judgement? She had to say something to stop them from looking at each other.

"I just don't know how my life got into such a mess in one day. I was fine before. I had a dull but steady job, and safe daydreams about an unobtainable older woman. I was doing okay."

Helen sighed and said, "No, love, you weren't. You were standing in one place, letting everything pass you by. Here's the thing, Zoe. If you do nothing, if you settle and then just stay dormant, stay still… then life pushes you along. It might not be a nice push. It might be a shove or a kick up the arse, but life pushes you along."

"Life didn't flippin' push me along. You and Jamie did."

"Yeah, and if we hadn't, something else would have happened. You would have gotten ill, won the lottery, been struck by lightning, started dating someone, or Darren's Book Nook would have gone under. Humans aren't made to just stay still; life happens and pushes you along. This time, it just used me and Jamie to do it."

"Very philosophical, Hel. I'm too tired for this though. I want to go home, have a hot shower, and go to sleep."

"You sure? It's really early and you didn't drink your tea," said Jamie, with a mug in his hand.

"Screw my tea. I'm having a shot of vanilla vodka before the shower and then another one just before bed. You drink the tea."

She saw Helen and Jamie exchange glances. Jamie put the tea down and kissed his sister on the crown of her head.

"I'll take you home and make sure you have a tall glass of water with that vodka," Helen offered.

"Thanks. And thank you for coming to get me, Jamie. I don't know what I'd do without you."

"Hey, what's family for? Just be careful and get some sleep. Everything will look better in the morning," Jamie promised.

She gave him a hug and left the apartment with Helen right behind her. She made a mental note to make it a large shot of vodka to dull her brain and bury this day.

CHAPTER FIFTEEN

Rebecca

Rebecca had woken up with a nervous energy coursing through her. Yesterday's meeting with Zoe and the kiss were buzzing around her mind and she blamed them for spilling her morning coffee. And for putting too much honey on her yoghurt. And for tripping over the cat. Most of all she blamed them for her lack of reaction to the fact that she didn't have a cat. Her neighbour's cat had come in through the open window and she hadn't thought twice about it until she tripped over the damn creature. Leading her to scold herself and wonder just how distracted a person could be.

Arriving at work, she willed herself to focus. She was Rebecca Clare. There was an expectation for her to be calm, controlled, and professional always. Not to be mooning over a woman who was about fifteen years younger than her and in the middle of a mental breakdown.

Rebecca's lack of social skills, when it came to anything but business negotiations and minor office disputes, meant that she didn't even know if it had been actual attraction or some form of misguided need for physical comfort that had driven Zoe to instigate a kiss. Should she call Zoe to find out? That sounded like an uncomfortable conversation to say the least.

She clamped her jaw tightly shut. Why do I have to be so useless when it comes to human interactions? I should stop thinking about her now.

She walked past reception, nodding and smiling at today's receptionists, hoping they hadn't heard about what happened yesterday. Hoping that tales of Rebecca Clare having an impromptu meeting with a crying woman in casual clothing, who then ended up running away from the building mere minutes after the meeting started, hadn't spread. Thank heavens they were British and too polite to ask any questions or she would have been mortified.

One of the receptionists stood up suddenly. "Oh, Ms. Clare. Excuse me but you have someone waiting for you here."

Rebecca stopped dead in her tracks. It was five past eight and her first meeting wasn't until ten fifteen. In fact, she wasn't supposed to be in the office until nine today. Who would be here waiting for her? Could it be Zoe?

"I do?"

She looked over to the seating area and saw two faces she recognized from an earlier visit.

Zoe's friend and her brother. This should be interesting. Or dreadful. Or both.

She fought to keep her expression neutral.

"Well, hello again and good morning. Would you like to come up to a meeting room? I'm assuming that our discussion needs privacy this time?" she asked the two staring faces.

"Uh, yeah. I suppose that would be best. We won't stay for long, though. We both have work to get to," the man answered. Rebecca struggled to remember his name. Was it James?

"Ah, that explains why you are here so early. That is a good thing as most of the meeting rooms should be free for the next half an hour or so. Would you like to come with me?" She began to walk to the turnstile to get the guard to let them all in.

***

After ordering a tray of coffee, tea and biscuits, Rebecca sat down and looked at her two guests. She was regretting choosing the small meeting room at the top of the stairs. Too many memories in here from yesterday. Memories of chestnut eyes brimming with tears, of nervous hands fidgeting with a cup of tea, and of full lips pressed forcefully against her own. That kiss had felt so good, despite the inappropriate circumstances.

"I'm sorry to barge in on you like this again but as Jamie and I were the ones to start this whole thing up, we felt like we should step in and try to fix this mess," Helen said.

Jamie, that's what he's called, Rebecca mused. I wonder what Zoe told them. How much do they know?

"I see. How is Zoe? I wanted to call her last night but I wasn't sure if she wanted some privacy?"

"What she wants is to not have been sacked and not have rushed into your building and kissed you," Jamie said.

Rebecca felt a freezing feeling in her chest. Zoe regretted their kiss. Of course she did. It had just been a need for distraction and comfort on her behalf. Zoe had never made a secret of the fact that she looked up to her and, heaven knows, she had tried to behave like a role model.

Like a mentor. Not like some skirt-chasing middle-aged man with a weakness for young women.

"Ah. She told you everything, then?" Rebecca asked, trying to keep the shame out of her voice.

"Yes," Helen said. Then her gaze flickered down to her hands.

Rebecca cleared her throat. "I want you both to know that I didn't intentionally encourage any… physical affection."

She hated how stilted and prim she sounded when she talked about things like this. It added ten years to her age, and that was the last thing she wanted to do when talking about Zoe and their situation.

Jamie sat forward on his chair. "No, no. We know. And Zoe feels awful about it. She's so sorry she put you through that."

Rebecca tried in vain to figure out what he was talking about, in the end she gave up and asked, "what?"

Jamie looked at her with a blank expression. "What?"

Helen looked from one to the other. "What?"

"What do you mean by 'put me through'?" Rebecca asked.

She was starting to feel stupid.

"Well, you know, pouncing on you," Helen said. There was a pink tinge covering her cheeks.

"Pouncing? No one pounced. We kissed," Rebecca said.

Helen and Jamie looked at each other and Rebecca sensed a silent conversation taking place between them.

"You mean you didn't feel attacked or freaked out?" Jamie asked.

"About what?"

Jamie stared at her before clarifying. "About the kiss?"

Rebecca grew uncomfortable. This was an odd enough situation on its own but discussing it with strangers was unpleasant to say the least.

"No, if I had, I wouldn't have taken part in it."

"You took part?" Helen exclaimed.

There was a knock on the door. It was the new receptionist bringing in the tray of refreshments. What was her name? Katherine? Kathryn? Katarina?... Mel? Rebecca tried to read the name tag but her long hair was draped over it.

"Thank you… dear."

"Of course, Ms. Clare. Anything else I can help you with?"

Yes, you can get lost so I can figure out what the hell is going on here, a voice in Rebecca's mind shouted.

"No, that'll be all. Thank you."

The receptionist left them with a nod and a smile. As soon as she was gone, Helen grabbed the sleeve of Rebecca's suit jacket.

"You mean the kiss was a two-way kiss?"

Rebecca tried not to bristle. This still felt strangely inappropriate.

"Well, yes. Zoe was upset. She seemed about to, well, snap in some way. We got close to each other and I wanted to comfort her and she seemed to need comfort. I was considering giving her a light hug or something. I just knew I needed to calm her down and stop her from spinning out of control. And then it… somehow turned into a kiss. Then, of course, she took off running before I could apologise."

They laughed. Both of these fidgety twentysomethings just laughed.

Jamie held up a hand. "Sorry, we're just relieved. You see, Zoe is convinced that you are not into her and that she pounced on you and kissed you against your will. She's felt so guilty. She's been crazy in love with you for ages and that kiss was sort of her reaching fever pitch and—"

He was interrupted by a clearly flustered Helen. "Jamie! You can't tell her that."

He seemed to realise what he had just said and looked from Helen to Rebecca open-mouthed before whispering, "Shit. I'm not supposed to tell you that she has a crush on you. Bugger, she's gonna kill me."

So many things happened inside Rebecca at once. The realisation that Zoe didn't think of her as a role model but as dating material, the fact that Zoe had apparently been "crazy in love" with her for ages and not just seeking a mentor as she had thought.

It was impossible for Rebecca to make her self-image of an emotionally repressed, dull, ginger woman who, at forty, was closer to middle-age than she wanted to admit, gel with someone that this fascinating, young beauty could fall for. All those times that Zoe had stared at her and Rebecca had assumed she was just shy or staring because Rebecca said something painfully uncool – could they have been looks of admiration?

Had that kiss been more than a kneejerk reaction from someone distraught?

Suddenly, it struck Rebecca that Jamie had said that Zoe was distressed because she felt she'd attacked her with that kiss. She felt distraught to think of Zoe so upset over a misunderstanding. Attacked? Could she really have missed how she had pushed her lips right back against Zoe's full, soft lips? Had she not heard the pathetic little whimper that escaped from Rebecca's mouth as she was finally kissed after going months without physical contact? After having fantasised about kissing Zoe so many times that she couldn't think about their Saturdays in Queenswell library without feeling all tingly.

"I have to speak to Zoe immediately. I have to let her know that the kiss was reciprocated and that she doesn't have to worry," Rebecca said. She was trying to sound collected and hated that her voice had cracked on that last word.

Jamie stood up and shook her hand. "Okay. Thank you. Just, um, is there any way you could, you know, not tell her that I told you about her crush? Maybe pretend like it never happened?"

"Of course. I know you didn't mean to tell me and I know that Zoe will certainly need a good relationship with her brother in the upcoming months."

"Oh, great, cheers for that. And thanks for not thinking it's weird that me and Helen are the ones to come to see you. You know, both back then and now."

"That's fine. The first time was a bit... unexpected. But this time I understand why it had to be you. I assume Zoe felt like she couldn't face me."

Rebecca stood up. "Anyway, I think I should be calling Zoe to put her mind at ease so unless you need anything else from me?"

"No, that's it. Man, I'm so relieved. Thanks again and take care," Jamie said with a warm smile that looked a lot like his sister's.

Rebecca shook their hands and walked them out, making polite small talk. Her mind wasn't concerned with them at all, however. It was full to the brim with thoughts of Zoe.

CHAPTER SIXTEEN

Rebecca

Rebecca was sitting at the table in the meeting room. It was still filled with the things from the refreshment tray that she, Jamie, and Helen had so successfully ignored. Her glasses were discarded next to one of the cups.

Her eyes were closed; the fingers of one hand pinching the bridge of her nose where her glasses always cut in and her other hand holding the mobile phone to her ear. She felt her heart beat hard with every signal that went through. And then she heard Zoe's clear-as-spring-water voice answer.

"Hi. Sorry I took a while to pick up. I couldn't find my phone."

Rebecca wasn't sure if that was true. Zoe sounded rushed and unsure of her own words.

"That's fine. I'm just calling to…" Rebecca stopped, unsure of how to approach this conversation. "I'm just calling to put your mind at ease," she finished.

"Put my mind at ease?"

"Yes. About the kiss."

Silence. Deep, indecipherable silence. Rebecca decided to press on.

"I wanted you to know that I…" She stopped again, cursing her brain for not cooperating. "I wanted you to know that I really enjoyed it. And that I… don't regret it and that I hope you don't either."

More silence. It gnawed on Rebecca's nerves now. Why wouldn't the woman just speak? Unable to stand the silence, Rebecca kept talking.

"Of course, I am sure you have bigger things to worry about, like your career and how you are going to pay the rent next month."

There was a quiet reply of "no." It sounded like it came from far away.

Then Zoe cleared her throat and added, "I have some savings. I should be fine for a couple of months. Three if I cut down on the fast food."

Rebecca felt as if she was about to get a killer headache. How could they be discussing food right now?

"I see. I'm glad you are not in dire straits."

"I'm glad that…" the clear voice on the line started to say but then went back to the thick silence.

"What? What made you glad, Zoe?"

Silence again. Rebecca counted her breaths to keep from losing her cool. One breath, two breaths, three breaths, four…

"That you called. That you liked the kiss. That I didn't offend or, y'know, violate you."

Rebecca almost laughed with relief. "Oh Zoe, no. You didn't violate me at all. You gave me what I've been wanting every single Saturday in that drafty library."

"Really? I… I wasn't sure."

"No. I can tell. Well, for the record, I gathered that you liked me but I was almost certain you didn't like me in a romantic fashion. I have always been bad at reading romantic intention, especially in those who aren't my obvious choices for partners," Rebecca said.

"Obvious choices?"

"Sorry, I should have explained that better. As I say, I'm not very good at this emotional stuff. I meant that if it's someone more like me in age and type and they figuratively hit me over the head with a bowl full of compliments. Anyone out of that narrow category and I'm useless."

"That's sort of how I felt too. You are so different from anyone I have ever dated," Zoe said softly.

Rebecca took a deep breath. "Well, then let's stop being so British and just come straight out with it. I like you. I admire you. I care about you. And I am painfully attracted to you."

"Painfully?"

Rebecca wasn't sure if the new tone in Zoe's uncertain voice was hope or playfulness, but it sounded happier and that was all she needed.

"Yes, painfully. Have you ever felt like you were objectifying a younger woman? You end up feeling like some dirty old man; I don't recommend it at all."

Zoe laughed. All deities and saints bless this woman for always laughing at my jokes.

"Does it help if I said I felt like a stupid teenage girl with a crush on a teacher?"

"Teenage girl? You're twenty-six. Besides, being kicked out by homophobic parents must have made you grow up very fast. I'd say you are older than your years."

Zoe hummed noncommittally. "Maybe in some ways. In other ways, I think I sort of stayed at eighteen."

"The woman I have gotten to know feels more mature than many who are my age."

"Good, then you shouldn't worry so much about our age gap. I mean, you know, if there is a possible 'us' to worry about."

Rebecca swallowed and tried to keep her tone light. "I'm not sure, Zoe. What do you think?"

"I'd like there to be an 'us' to worry about some day."

"In that case, start worrying."

"One step ahead of you," Zoe replied, her voice chiming with laughter.

Rebecca felt the corners of her lips tug into a broad smile. Her eyes were still closed but her fingers weren't rubbing the bridge of her nose anymore. Instead her hand rested on her chest, where under her favourite, designer shirt she could feel her heart pound. This all felt so sudden and she wasn't sure she could keep up with the quick pace. She realised that she didn't care if she wasn't in control of this. What did it matter? She felt happy and that hadn't happened in such a long time.

"I… don't know what happens now," Zoe said, breaking her out of her reverie.

"Neither do I. And that is a situation I am not used to."

"This kinda changes everything, doesn't it?"

Rebecca opened her eyes and looked at the small meeting room, which suddenly seemed so much more welcoming than before.

"Yes. Yes, I think it does," she answered.

"Before Jamie and Helen went to see you, I hadn't had any real change since I broke up with my last girlfriend years ago. I'd sort of avoided it."

"Do you wish you could have avoided this?"

"Hmm. Being sacked from my job like that? Yes. Meeting you? Hell no."

Rebecca smiled to herself. "That's the thing about change, in my experience there is a fifty per cent chance of it being negative but just as big a chance that it will be positive."

"Yeah. I suppose I shouldn't try to stay away from change."

"No. There's really no point. Even if you refrain from taking any form of action... your surroundings will stay in motion and not let you stay still, Zoe."

Zoe sighed over the telephone line.

"Yeah. Helen said something like that. She said that no matter how hard you try to not let anything change, life pushes you along."

"She's a clever girl."

"She's my age. She's a woman, not a girl," Zoe corrected, sounding slightly terse.

"Right. Of course. It was just an expression. Trust me, I know that you are all woman."

She was rewarded with Zoe's laughter again.

"Uh-huh. Checked that out, have you?" Zoe asked, tone full of mischief.

"What red-blooded person wouldn't? Have you seen yourself?"

Rebecca realised how good it felt to flirt again, and how good it felt to flirt with someone who was going to be more than a brief holiday romance.

"I'd rather be looking at you. In fact, I can't wait to see you again. Especially now that... everything is different," Zoe said.

"I know what you mean. Seeing you will be a completely different experience now. No more wondering. No more walking on eggshells so I don't accidentally make you uncomfortable. No trying to gauge your interest at any given moment."

"Exactly. Now it will just be… first date nerves, I suppose?"

"Hmm. Yes, I suppose so. Are we calling it a first date?"

The line went quiet and Rebecca was just about to ask Zoe if she was still there when she heard her say, "I'd like it to be a date, yes. Would you?"

"Absolutely," Rebecca replied. She could hear the purr in her own voice and had to remind herself to tone it down. This was all so new and Zoe was in such a vulnerable state. She had to let Zoe lead and decide the pace; she found that she was quite enamoured with that idea.

"Great. So, um, do you want to go do something special or…" Zoe trailed off, sounding hesitant.

"Or meet up at the library and look for new jobs for you? I'll let you choose. Either sounds great to me. I just want to see you again."

"Well, I don't want to waste out first date on work stuff. Or take advantage of the fact that I'm dating my job coach. Can I take you out for a casual dinner tonight?"

"Only if you let me help you job search on Saturday."

"It's a deal."

CHAPTER SEVENTEEN

Rebecca

Rebecca wondered if the restaurant was a good choice. Was it too posh? Zoe had asked her to choose a place and she had. But now she saw Zoe fidget and glance around at the surroundings and she wondered if she should have picked somewhere else.

"Is this okay? We can go somewhere else if you'd like?"

"What? No, no this is fine. I'm just… a little nervous."

Ah, it's not the place that disconcerts her, it's me.

Rebecca smoothed a napkin on her lap, smiled at Zoe, and tried to sound reassuring as she said, "Don't be. Just think of it as one of our job search sessions."

Zoe gave a mix of a scoff and a laugh and Rebecca spotted that cute little crooked tooth in her lower jaw.

"I was nervous then too."

"Worse than this?" Rebecca asked and took a sip of her wine.

Zoe tucked some of her thick, black curls behind her ear.

"No, it's just different this time. Now I'm nervous because I think you'll come to your senses and realise that you are out of my league."

"Oh good. Then we are sitting here afraid of the same thing. We can be anxious, insecure idiots together."

Zoe laughed. "Wow, I really know how to show a girl a good time, huh?"

Rebecca tried for a teasing tone of voice. "I thought we were sticking to the word 'woman' and not 'girl?' Or is that just a rule for me?"

"No. No, I suppose I should stick to that too," Zoe replied, mirth flashing in her eyes.

The way Zoe was looking at her now was making Rebecca experience a mix of butterflies in her stomach and the heady pull of arousal emanating from her lower abdomen and sinking lower.

Rebecca cleared her throat. "You look less nervous now. Perhaps I just need to keep you talking?"

"Yeah. It's hard to think about anything else than how stunning and brilliant you are as soon as you open your mouth," Zoe replied.

"Are you referring to my intelligence when you hear me speak or was that a flirtatious way of saying that you like watching my lips part?"

With that, Rebecca had taken back the lead in this flirting game of theirs. She saw Zoe swallow visibly.

"Wow, you really are in another league to me," Zoe said, sounding almost reverent.

"Not at all, darling. I've just got a few years' extra experience."

Rebecca wondered if the restaurant was warm or if it was just her.

Zoe took a big gulp of her wine. Rebecca was happy with the wine she had chosen for them. The restaurant was mid-ranged when it came to prices and she had practically begged Zoe to let her pay. This meant that she had chosen the most expensive bottle of wine on the menu for them with a clear conscience. The claret was velvety and potent, and Rebecca hoped it would relax Zoe, as it had her.

A waiter came over, bringing their food. Zoe began arranging her plate, pushing her lettuce to the side and cutting her lasagne into small pieces. She ate some and made a moaning noise in appreciation.

"Please don't do that," Rebecca said before she could stop herself.

"Oh sorry. My table manners have always been awful."

"It's not that," she quickly reassured. "It's just that my mind seems to be in the gutter enough without you helping it further down by making... delicious noises. Not that it's your fault of course. I can just feel my self-control slipping a little tonight so I'm trying to catch hold of it."

"Why?" Zoe asked.

"Pardon?"

"Why? Don't control yourself. I really like the way you keep looking at me like I'm your dessert."

Rebecca felt her cheeks flush. Surely the restaurant must be hot, it couldn't just be her burning up like this. She looked at Zoe, all cleavage and long eyelashes batting slowly, and decided that it was probably all her and the restaurant was quite possibly cold as ice.

"Well, you certainly look like dessert. Does your shirt have to be so unbuttoned? I'm finding it hard to breathe."

"That's your problem. I don't have as fancy clothes as you so I have to play to my strengths – my curves."

At the word curves, Zoe ran the back of her fingers over her cleavage. Quickly and subtly caressing the shimmering skin in a way which made Rebecca feel dizzy.

"Nice to see that you got over your nervousness."

"It's still lurking at the back of my head. You staring at me is making it hide more and more though, so please keep ogling," Zoe said, blinking those long-lashed, flirty eyes once more. Then, as if that nervousness came back as it heard itself mentioned, Zoe quickly looked down and continued eating.

Rebecca couldn't make this woman out. One moment Zoe was all confidence and flirtation, the next she was a shy flower in need of tending. It was confusing. It was sweet. It was irresistible.

Rebecca had to ask.

"Why is it so hot in here?"

Zoe smirked. "Is this my queue to drop a cheesy line and say that it's not the place, it's you? Because you are smoking-hot tonight. That dress must be oozing with gratitude for being allowed to hug your body that tight."

Rebecca laughed. "Jealous of it?"

Zoe's chestnut-coloured eyes looked suddenly serious. "Hell yes."

Heat coursed through Rebecca. Oh god, she just got even sexier. How am I supposed to be the experienced and suave one here when she can make me burn for her so easily. Stop looking at me like that!

Out loud, she simply cleared her throat before focusing on her sirloin steak. She chewed and swallowed the perfectly cut pieces, but barely tasted it. This date was not going the way it should. They should be getting to know each other and enjoying some relaxed banter and small talk. Instead, they were locked in a circle of uncomfortable nervousness and unbridled lust. Going around and around. She had never been on a date like this before. But then, she had never had a romantic entanglement that started the way this one had. Her romances were always calculated and calm things,

116

steered by both her and the man or woman she was dating. This however, was a car without a driver, swaying across the road much too fast.

"Are you okay?" Zoe asked.

"Yes. Well, yes and no. This date is just a little unconventional for me."

"How so?" Zoe asked, brow furrowed.

"Normally at this stage of a date I'm thinking about what clever questions to ask or how to portray myself in a good light. Right now, however, I'm deciding between what needs my focus more. Is it trying to keep us both relaxed and comfortable or keeping from launching myself across the table and kissing your brains out."

Zoe smirked again. "I think I like our date better then." She pushed her half-empty plate away. "I'm done. So, whenever the waiter comes back, feel free to pay and then let's go find a black cab."

"A taxi?"

"Yes, to some place where you can kiss my brains out without having to worry about people staring. I don't mind public displays of affection but I have a feeling you are more private."

Rebecca wondered if she looked funny in her state of shock. Was her mouth open? Her eyes wide? "Um, well, yes. I am."

"Great. So, finish your food, pay the bill and then let's go get a cab. Sound good?"

Rebecca pushed her plate away, even though she had only eaten a few bites.

"Sounds perfect."

***

The taxi ride had been unbearable. They sat together in the backseat after giving Rebecca's home address as their destination. Zoe had been casting furtive glances at her when the driver wasn't looking. Glances brimming with promise.

Rebecca returned the looks and found herself staring at this fascinating and beautiful woman with pitch-black curls almost down to her shoulders, impressively smooth light brown skin, high cheekbones, and a smile which normally looked mischievous but, in this sexually-loaded situation, looked downright wicked.

It was so hard not to reach out and touch that smooth skin or to kiss those lips that tonight glistened with burgundy lipstick.

When Rebecca sat forward a little to give the cab driver further directions to her Marylebone flat, she had felt Zoe's hand caress along her thigh. It stopped just at the edge of her dress and then slowly, so painfully slowly, slid under it to snake further up.

Rebecca knew that the cab driver couldn't see what was happening below her waistline but that hand pushing its way under her tight dress still made her feel exposed and painfully aroused at the same time.

After what felt like an age, they arrived at her flat. Rebecca hurried to pay and then to rush inside and towards the elevator. Zoe followed at a slower pace. She was almost stalking, hips swaying, wicked grin in place.

She's the hunter and I feel like the prey. I'm older and more experienced, but I'm certainly not in charge.

Suddenly, Zoe's smirk turned into an open-mouthed smile and Rebecca saw that small, crooked tooth that she found so endearing. Affection muddled her lust and she no longer cared who was meant to be in charge. All she wanted was to get her tongue into that beautiful mouth.

"Come here," she said in a low purr.

She pulled Zoe into the lift and pushed the button for Level Six. Then she kissed her. It was nothing like that kiss they had in the meeting room. Nothing like that kiss when Zoe had been on the brink of a nervous breakdown. There was no crisis, no panic, no anxiety. It was a languid, soft, warm joining of two eager mouths. Tongue, lips, and teeth all moulded together and moved around each other as if they had been kissing like this for years.

Whatever suave collectedness their mouths had, their hands lacked. They both pawed and grabbed at each other as if they were only allowed a few minutes of touching and were making the most of it. Rebecca groaned filthily as her hands cupped Zoe's breasts under the leather jacket. Zoe instantly replied by arching her back, pushing her breasts deeper into Rebecca's grip. It was impossible to say who was more willing, they were perfectly in sync when it came to their need.

Getting the keys to the front door out of her handbag seemed an impossible task with Zoe kissing her neck and gripping her hips from behind, but she managed it in the end. Moaning in the most unladylike way, Rebecca led them into the apartment and towards the bedroom.

She felt Zoe tugging at her dress and part of her wanted Zoe to just pull, tear, and rip it off her. She couldn't stand the idea of fabric separating them.

She clumsily took the dress off while trying to kiss Zoe and finally managed to stand in front of her new lover in only her underwear. Zoe looked her up and down and Rebecca felt her clit twitch and harden, she was getting hopelessly wet and needed Zoe right now.

She didn't have to wait, Zoe kneeled before her and yanked her knickers down in one desperate tug. The garment was tight and the pull should have hurt, but she barely felt it. She did feel the cool air hitting her overheated sex and she felt the intense looks from the beautiful woman kneeling in front of her.

There was so much she wanted to do, undress Zoe, kiss every inch of her, feel Zoe's hands roam her body and possibly her mouth following cue but it all vanished in a haze of pleasure as she felt Zoe's mouth where she needed it the most. Warm wetness met warm wetness and Zoe's clever tongue chased away all thoughts from Rebecca's mind. She took hold of Zoe's hair and pulled her closer to her sex. Moaning her name, without a trace of her normal self-control. She didn't care. For once in her life – Rebecca Clare didn't mind not being in control of herself.

CHAPTER EIGHTEEN

Zoe

Zoe breathed in deep through her nose. The room smelled of Rebecca. Well, it foremost smelled of sex and of their mingled perfumes, but underneath that she could smell Rebecca's natural scent on the bedding and obviously on the woman lying on the pillow next to her.

They were on their sides, facing each other and Rebecca looked... different. The light from the bedside lamp, which Rebecca had switched on when they had finished making love, showed that Rebecca's usually precise eye makeup was smudged, her lipstick was kissed away, and her hair mussed-up.

Zoe could see the freckles and slight wrinkles that Rebecca usually hid with makeup. She also saw the warm smile and the searching look of those blue-green eyes. Rebecca looked vulnerable, sweet, and unbelievably beautiful. Zoe's heart wouldn't stop hammering at the sight of her.

"You are so bloody gorgeous. You should have been a model or something. Why are you looking at me like that, though?" she asked Rebecca.

"Like what?"

Rebecca's voice was croaky and her brow furrowed at the question.

"Like you're looking for something," Zoe explained.

"Perhaps I am. Perhaps I'm wondering what you are thinking?"

"Why not ask me, then? That's easier, isn't it?"

Rebecca rolled her eyes.

"Fine. What are you thinking?"

"Honestly? I was admiring that pretty face of yours. And deciding that your bed smells nice," Zoe answered.

Rebecca's smirk was downright dirty. "It does now. I'm surprised you aren't dehydrated after that."

Zoe knew it was ridiculous but the comment made her self-conscious. She had never been a very confident lover, not even with Rebecca, who had made her so very bold a few hours ago when they crashed through the front door.

"Oh darling, please don't look sad. That was a compliment. Not all women can achieve that, you know. Some even say it's a myth," Rebecca said with a purr in her voice.

Zoe reached out and pinched Rebecca's upper arm. It was childish but it was all she could muster right now.

"Stop saying 'that' in that tone of voice. Can we change the topic?" she asked, noting how grumpy she sounded.

"Of course, my sweet. How about we try for some sleep? If you want to stay the night, I mean? I understand if you want to get home to your own bed."

Zoe scrunched up her nose. "My bed doesn't have you in it. It's a flaw that damn bed has suffered from for ages. I'll stay here, if you don't mind."

Rebecca smiled and Zoe thought she saw relief in that smile.

"I don't mind at all. As long as you don't snore, that is."

"I don't. But I do sleepwalk sometimes."

"I'll make sure to keep you here with me," Rebecca whispered.

She moved forward, so close that Zoe felt her breath against her face. Under the duvet, Zoe felt her hands slide in place. One arm in the space between Zoe's waist and the bed and the other one on Zoe's hip. They were so close now that under the press of breasts against breasts, Zoe could feel Rebecca's heartbeat. It started slow, but as they laid so close and looked into each other's eyes, it quickened.

"Yeah, that should keep me from wandering off. I'm just gonna nick a kiss before sleep if that's all right?" Zoe asked, surprised at how hoarse she suddenly sounded.

"Go ahead," Rebecca breathed against her lips.

Zoe leaned in for a kiss. She could taste the tiniest hint of salt on Rebecca's heart-shaped lips and knew it came from her. Some of her was now a part of Rebecca and vice versa. It was a daunting and yet comforting thought. Most of all, it was intoxicating. Just a few weeks ago, she hadn't dared to think that Rebecca Clare would even learn her name and now... well, now she could taste her own sex on Rebecca's lips. She knew what Rebecca looked like in the throes of passion. She knew how Rebecca liked to be touched and what she was uncomfortable with. Most of all, she knew what it felt like to see Rebecca look at her like she was right now. Like she was a miracle.

Zoe smiled and closed her eyes to sleep, knowing full well that despite her physical exhaustion, she wasn't going to go to sleep for a long time. But trying felt nice. Trying to sleep with Rebecca holding her, and breathing on her, and oh-so-softly whispering, "Goodnight my beautiful darling."

CHAPTER NINETEEN

Zoe

The next day Zoe went home when Rebecca left for work. The trip to Queenswell seemed to sail by; she felt like she was floating and wasn't even bothered by walking in pigeon poo at the station. When she got home she showered, ate, caught up on the sleep she had missed, and, in between all of this, texted Rebecca.

It was amazing how many silly reasons she could think up to text Rebecca. It was even more amazing that Rebecca replied to each one as if it had been completely valid and important. Zoe wondered how much work Rebecca was missing due to those texts but considering Rebecca's replies – she certainly didn't seem to mind.

As soon as it was past six, Zoe rushed out of her flat and went to see Jamie. She knew he'd be home by then. He let her in on the first knock and Zoe was surprised to see Helen there.

"Oi, what are you doing here?"

"Finished early at work today. Don't worry, I haven't been sacked like you."

Zoe rolled her eyes. "Charming." She sat down on the threadbare sofa. "It must have been really early if you had time to shower and then come over here. Cuz you've either showered or you're trying out the wet look with your hair. If you are – it's not working for ya, love."

Jamie and Helen glanced at each other.

"I caught that look. What?"

"Um, well, you've been really busy with the work stuff and the Rebecca stuff so we might have forgotten to tell you..." Helen said.

She fidgeted with her hair but didn't seem to be willing to continue the sentence. Jamie stepped forward instead.

"Shit, Zoe. We forgot to tell you that we moved in together."

"You what?" Zoe exclaimed.

"Moved in together," Jamie said, smiling this time.

"Uh. Okay. When?"

Helen sat down next to her, at the very edge of the sofa.

"A few days ago. You're not mad that we didn't tell you, are you?"

"Hel. Is it like me to be mad at something like that?"

"No. It's not. But I know you haven't always been thrilled that your brother and best friend were dating," Helen said with a look of embarrassment.

"Nah. I mean, yes it's weird but I'm used to it. I mean, it's kinda strange that you two moved in together so fast. "

Jamie gave a loud, incredulous scoff.

"We've been together for two years, you flippin' nuisance."

Zoe just grinned at him. Next to her, Helen sighed.

"Jamie. When will you learn that she's taking the piss out of you? Just leave it."

He crossed his arms. "Yeah? You wanna play it like that, Sis? Well, guess what? I know something you don't."

Zoe saw Helen look at him in bewilderment.

"Uh-huh. Is it the magical trick of losing all your money on online blackjack?"

He stamped his foot like a child before saying, "Once, Zoe. That happened once!"

She had him going now and it was far too much fun. It had been a long time since she enjoyed winding him up like this. Everything was more fun today.

"Okay. So, that's not it? What on earth is it you know that I don't, big brother?"

He looked smug. "Your Rebecca."

"Yes? What about her?" Zoe asked.

Her pulse had picked up. Did Jamie know about them spending the night together?

"When she leaves work today and you go and meet her. She said you'd planned to meet up in London tonight? Well, when you do. She'll have a surprise for you. From Darren."

"WHAT?"

Zoe's outburst made Jamie look taken aback. He did the lip biting thing he always did when he said too much.

"Shit. I probably shouldn't have told you that. She wanted to surprise you. She just wanted me and Helen to know because she assumed, and she was right in this, that we'd be bloody furious with him for what he said to you."

"Surprise me how, Jamie? Tell me!"

He rubbed his face with his hand while groaning.

"Just tell us. You have said this much, you might as well carry on," Helen said.

"Bloody bollocks, why do I always do this?" he said before removing his hand from his face and continuing. "She said that she went to see Darren during her lunch hour. She said that the shop already looked a bit messy and that he looked stressed as hell. Still, she gave him a piece of her mind and threatened to bring a solicitor friend of hers into this. Apparently, he caved like a house of cards, and she has an envelope that contains a written apology and some money, I think?"

Zoe felt so many things at once and wasn't quite sure where to start. "Money? What did she do? Blackmail him?"

"Well, no. I mean, I don't know. Ask her! Go see her tonight and ask her."

Zoe stood up. "I can do better than that. I'm going to call her right now."

Without saying goodbye, she stormed towards the door. She took her phone out of her pocket and looked for Rebecca's number as she closed the door behind her and headed for the stairs.

When Rebecca answered, Zoe was running down the stairs with echoing footfalls.

Rebecca's voice sounded warm and happy as she said hello. Zoe was too confused to reply in kind.

"Yeah, hey, it's me. What the hell did you say to Darren? What's happened?"

"Ah. Jamie spoke to you. Damn. I wish he hadn't. I really wanted to sit down together and explain," Rebecca replied.

Zoe was getting out of breath but somehow it felt good to be on the move during this conversation.

"Yeah, well, explain it now."

"All right. I went to see Darren. I spoke to him about how the two of you had left things and that it was unacceptable for him to treat you that way. I… might have mentioned an acquaintance who specialises in professional disputes and explained to him the sort of situation he would be in if you decided to be less understanding than you have been. At the end of our chat he was quite agreeable."

Zoe had stopped at the bottom of the stairs, feeling her anger slowly ebbing. *Am I overreacting? Should I be happy she wanted to surprise me by doing something nice for me?*

"Yeah, I bet he was. Go on."

"He has agreed to pay your last pay check and add a settlement payment as a well-earned bonus and a thank you for not taking this to court or to the press. I also assisted him in writing an honest, and therefore positive, reference letter for you."

Zoe took a deep breath, trying to calm her pounding heart.

"That was very kind of you and I really, really appreciate the money and the fact that you taught him a lesson so he won't behave like this to someone else, but Rebecca—"

"But I should have asked you before talking to him after you made it clear that you wanted him out of your life?" Rebecca interrupted.

"Yeah."

"I knew there was a risk you'd see it like that. But Zoe, I couldn't let him get away with treating you like that. You were the heart, soul, and brain of that place and you gave it so many years of your life. The things he said would have been unforgivable no matter who it was directed at, but at you, well, that couldn't stand. I didn't ask your permission because I knew you would have just let it go, because you are too sweet and you don't value yourself enough to stand up to someone like him. So, I took a risk, hoping that, with time, you would see that I had to do something. I am sincerely sorry if I upset you and I will try to never do that again. But Zoe, he had to be stopped."

She saw Rebecca's point. There was still that uncomfortable feeling in the pit of her stomach, though. It screamed that she could look after herself and that no one should make decisions for her. It screamed that she could only rely on herself. Her brain was deciding to join the conversation now. Maybe someone who will help me do the things I can't or don't want to do is a good thing? Maybe I should just trust her to want what is best for me? Maybe I should give her a chance?

She breathed through her nose and didn't answer Rebecca until her breathing was calm, and her brain and gut instinct had settled on a solution.

"I see what you were trying to do. And yeah, I get why you didn't ask me. But I need to make this clear, no matter if it's best for me or not – I need you to always check with me in the future. If I want to drop it, we both drop it. Okay?"

"Of course. I see now how my decision to do this without checking with you first was ill-advised. I focused too much on wanting justice for you, and I stepped all over one of my favourite things about you: your independence. I apologise. I'm just used to taking charge and doing what needs to be done. I'll have to temper that."

Zoe smiled as she sighed.

"Yeah. I think we both have to do some soul-searching and some work if we are going to be in a relationship."

"Anything that needs to be done, I am ready to do it. I want you in my life and I'll make any changes I need to in order to make you want to stay."

"That is so sweet. Oh, and I'll do that too, of course," Zoe said.

She stretched her muscles, tense from anger and running.

"Good. When I see you, I'll give you the cheque for the money and the USB stick with the word document file containing your glowing reference letter. Will that be tonight? That I see you, I mean?" Rebecca asked carefully.

"Yep, I haven't changed my mind, love. I'll see you tonight." She laughed. "Maybe in a few hours I will have recovered from the shock of all of that."

"I hope so. Although, you do have the most adorable shocked face."

Zoe frowned. "When have you seen my shocked face?"

Now it was Rebecca's turn to laugh.

"Hmm, let's see. What about that day when I told you that I had dated women and you looked like I had just given you a cheque for a million pounds?"

Zoe felt her jaw drop.

"Oh bugger! Was it that obvious? God, I'm so embarrassed."

Rebecca's warm laugh rang out again. "Oh, don't be, darling. It was the loveliest moment and I had to fight to not lean forwards and kiss you. I only stopped myself when I realised that you might be happy to have a gay mentor, not to have a possible love interest. If that makes sense?"

"Mm hmm. That makes sense. I'm so glad we don't have to wonder anymore."

"Me too. I'm so happy and proud that you want to be with me, darling."

"I feel the same way," Zoe said.

"Good, then leave for London whenever you're ready. I will get out of work early. Just let me know when you are here and I will come running. Or at least power walking with as much dignity as I can muster."

"Just don't fall in those high heels."

"Why not? If I do, you'll have to catch me," Rebecca replied.

"Whoa, you really are good at this flirting stuff."

"As I have said before, it's just experience. You'll catch up in no time."

"I hope so, gorgeous."

"Oh, I'll teach you everything I know," Rebecca promised.

"Well, in that case, I'll get on the train right away!"

"Good. Hurry."

"I will," Zoe replied.

She said goodbye and hung up with the biggest smile on her face. She couldn't believe that she had been through a whole range of emotions in just a few minutes. Clearly, loving Rebecca Clare was going to be anything but boring. Life pushes you along, indeed.

CHAPTER TWENTY

It was another cold but sunny Saturday. Zoe and Rebecca walked into the library, but this time, they were walking hand-in-hand. Zoe felt her chest fill with pride at the feel of Rebecca's slender fingers interlaced with her own.

They went into the reference room and sat down where they had always sat. The windows had been cleaned and the white light of the winter sun glinted off the top of Rebecca's head, giving her copper red hair a halo of light.

Zoe was just about to make a joke about her looking like an angel when Rebecca gave her a theatrical glare.

"Well? Are you just going to stare at me or are you going to get stuck in to the job search?"

"Yes, job coach! However, this time I am the one who has done some homework. I saw something promising last time I was at your place. There's a bookshop between Marylebone and Paddington and they had an ad in the window for a weekend supervisor. It's a higher post but with the great reference from Darren and your coaching for the interview, maybe I can pull it off?"

Rebecca's face lit up.

"Of course you can. With your reference letter, your spruced-up CV, and the application letter we can write you, you'll be a shoe-in to get to the interview stage. And when you get to that, your intelligence and charisma will do the rest."

"My charisma?"

Rebecca looked at her. "Yes, darling. Your charisma. You do know that your looks, mannerisms, and way of connecting with people can charm just about anyone?"

Zoe felt as if her world was being remapped.

"I'm charming?"

Rebecca looked at her, almost pityingly.

"Clearly the first thing we need to work on is your low self-esteem."

Zoe bit her lip, the pain helping her think.

"Well, if I get the job, I'm sure that will do the trick. You agreeing to date me is definitely doing wonders for my self-esteem."

A line formed between Rebecca's brows.

"I'd say I've done more than agree to date you, Zoe."

"Huh?"

"I want to make it very clear that I am in this for the long-term. I want to try to make a future with you. I'm not at the age where I want to casually date. I know you are fourteen years younger than I am and maybe you want something else here?" Rebecca said before pausing.

She took her glasses off and leaned in closer to Zoe.

"One of the reasons I assumed you weren't romantically interested in me at first, was that you might want to build a new life. Maybe travel a lot and settle down abroad. Or perhaps have children? Neither of those paths looked like what I have pictured for myself, and at my age you become less flexible with your future."

Zoe surveyed her. Did she say fourteen years younger? I can finally do the math. So, she's forty-years-old then? Thank heavens that came up without me having to ask.

"Sorry, gorgeous, but I've got to ask… are you nuts? I'm the woman who stayed in one spot and lived the same safe, uneventful life for almost a decade. Why would I want to travel and have a bunch of kids suddenly?"

"Because you have woken up from the slumber that your fear and inertia put you into. You are just starting to spread your wings and take flight. Being with me would tether you down."

"Good! It's bloody scary up here in the air. I want an anchor keeping me from getting lost and ending up in space… or in Yorkshire. Besides, you were the one who helped me fly when I was pushed out of the nest, so you'll be the one helping me buff up my feathers and figure out which direction I'm meant to fly in. Man, this analogy is rubbish. Can I have another one?"

Rebecca laughed.

"Have all the analogies you want, darling. I just want to make sure that you are happy to be with an older woman who already has a life all set up. Because being my romantic partner means just that, agreeing to a partnership. We wouldn't be dating; we would be at the start of a relationship."

"Brilliant. I need something solid now that the ground has disappeared beneath my feet. A steady relationship with someone who already has a built-up life is exactly what I want," Zoe said, startled at how fast and easy that reply had come to her.

Rebecca sat back, the worry line between her eyes gone.

"It's settled then?"

Zoe kept from whooping or cheering but felt her face crack into a beaming grin as she answered, "Yep. You're officially my girlfriend."

Zoe looked at the elegant, dignified, and apparently forty-year-old woman in front of her and realised that 'girlfriend' wasn't a fitting term here. *I'll just have to ask her to marry me one day. She looks much more like a fiancée than a girlfriend.* Zoe almost jumped out of her seat and quieted her premature thoughts as quickly as she could.

Rebecca smiled and put her glasses back on.

"I'll wear that title with pride, my love. Now. Shall we get back to the task of getting you that job?"

My love. Does that mean that she loves me? Is she getting close to saying that she loves me? the premature thoughts piped up. Zoe pushed her thoughts down, berating them as you would an overexcited puppy that is at risk of harming itself and everyone in the surroundings.

"Yeah. Let's get back to that," Zoe replied.

On the outside, she was serious now, listening to Rebecca while trying for a mature, focused look. On the inside, she was thrilled to bits. Rebecca was with her now and she wanted it to be long-term. She couldn't believe her luck and felt glad to know that this was one big change in her life that she didn't fear at all. In fact, she could barely wait.

CHAPTER TWENTY-ONE

Helen

Monday night found Helen, Zoe, and Rebecca sitting at the table in Jamie's little flat. They were chatting while Jamie was putting the finishing touches to dinner.

Helen had convinced Jamie that they should all have dinner together to belatedly celebrate the two of them moving in together and tonight was the first night they had all been free. Helen figured it was going to be a great chance to see if Rebecca was making her best friend happy.

"Zoe, did you pop into that bookshop with your application and stuff?" Helen asked while re-filling their glasses with wine.

Zoe blew out a breath.

"Yep. I went in there this morning. Now we just cross our fingers that they call me in for an interview."

"I'm certain they will," Rebecca said.

She put her hand over Zoe's on the table and Helen didn't miss the look on Zoe's face. It started as a small smile which grew until her face was a perfect picture of bliss.

It warmed Helen's heart and she had to remind herself not to get too sappy. At least not until she was drunk. Then all bets were off.

Jamie came in with little pots and pans filled with tapas dishes and they all tucked in.

After spending some time eating and complimenting Jamie's cooking until he started to look too smug, Helen caught Rebecca's eye and changed the topic.

"We all know what is going on with Zoe's job situation and I've bored you with details about mine and Jamie's. What about you? What's your job like?"

Rebecca neatly and soundlessly put her cutlery down on her plate. "I suppose it's often repetitive, but once in a while a challenge comes along and makes it worth it. Plus, I get to raise the confidence of the nice employees and trim the egos of the unpleasant ones. That's always a bonus. I may not be a people person but I'm brilliant at playing god with who gets praise and who has to re-do their latest report."

Zoe rolled her eyes. "She's not that tough with them. I've met some of the people who work for her when I've gone to pick her up and they all seem to love her."

Rebecca waved that comment away and proceeded to explain exactly what her job entailed. Helen had only asked to be polite but was finding herself really interested as she listened. There was an interesting woman under that proper, cool exterior. Rebecca was getting more and more animated as she described the boring bits of the job and how she had perfected ways of delegating them.

She had a wicked sense of humour and it was impossible not to laugh. Especially when Zoe would add in little snarky comments to make the tales even funnier. They made quite the team, Helen realised.

The night progressed and the conversation flowed easily. Nerves relaxed and jokes became less filtered while stories became more honest. Soon Rebecca fitted in as if she had always had a seat at their dinner table.

They listened as Jamie and Zoe told stories about their childhood, everything from friendly tree climbing to vicious play fights.

Helen sipped at her wine and surreptitiously examined the adoring way Rebecca looked at Zoe. Helen was no expert but it looked like a hell of a lot more than infatuation. She nodded to herself. Good, I think this might just last.

Then they got to the dark part of the Achidi past – Zoe being thrown out.

Zoe looked deep into her wine glass, one hand gripping it tightly. "So, yeah. As if they weren't freaked out enough about me being a tree climbing tomboy, I had to tell them that I was a lesbian. Suddenly they couldn't stand to look at me. I had to sit through hours of them asking questions, trying to convince me that I was just scared of boys or that I hadn't tried hard enough to like blokes. They seemed so bloody angry. But now, I think they were actually more disappointed and confused. Scared that I had condemned myself to hell just to rebel against them or something."

"They still think that. I can't stand it when they ask me if you have 'come to your senses' yet. It makes me want to shake them," muttered Jamie.

Helen watched as Zoe swallowed and slowly moved her hand from her wineglass, over the table and then on to rest on her brother's hand. He took it and squeezed.

Helen hated this. She never knew what to say to help the two people she loved most when this topic came up. Helpless and furious at Mr. and Mrs. Achidi, she tried to think of something that could help. Maybe it would have been easier if she was sober.

Rebecca cleared her throat. "I've found that sometimes blood isn't enough. Sometimes even love isn't enough. Prejudice or religion or fear can be stronger. There is nothing you can do about it but grieve for the injustice and try to move on."

She stopped, as if unsure if she should continue. Zoe looked at her with what seemed to be pleading and Rebecca carried on speaking.

"I'm not sure if it will be any comfort, but as someone who was adopted, I can tell you that family isn't about who is related to you by blood. It's about who will be there for you even when it is not easy to be. It's about who will be happy when you are happy. And it's about people who will be willing to put your needs before theirs, knowing that you will do the same for them. You can find a family other than the one you were born into. And not counting your brother, who you already had with you, I would say that you have found yourself a new family right here with us. We're all proud of you and we all believe in you, even when you don't."

Jamie shot Rebecca an appreciative look. "Couldn't have said it better myself." He moved his gaze to Zoe. "You crashed and burned, Sis. But from all that crap from our parents and from getting fired, has come something that you needed - a new support system. And you best believe that we're never gonna let you settle for less than you deserve again."

Helen had to stop herself from jumping up and hugging him. Instead she looked over at Zoe and added, "we love you, and everything you are. You are just as much my family as my parents. It's been like that since we were six. And I'd do anything for you, even when you're being a muppet. You know that, right?"

Zoe was teary-eyed and swallowed loudly.

"Thanks, everyone. I'll just say one thing before this gets sappier than bloody treacle… Now that I've gotten my life moving again, I promise to be a less self-centred sister to you Jamie. A less whingey friend to you, Hel. And I promise to make sure that you are never bored with your life again, babe." After the last word, Zoe leaned in and kissed Rebecca, whose cheeks reddened at the public display of affection.

Helen held up her almost empty glass to Zoe as to toast her. "Well, I told you didn't I, you silly sausage. Didn't I say that life would push you along?"

Zoe poked her tongue out at her. "Yep, but there's no way that you could have known that the direction it was gonna push me in would be this brilliant."

Helen emptied her glass and shrugged, trying not to look as smug as she felt. "Maybe not. But I'm still claiming it as a win."

"I think we're all winners right now. And that is rare in life so let's enjoy it," Rebecca said with a laugh.

She took Zoe's hand just as Helen felt Jamie put his hand on her knee.

Yes, Helen realised. Life had pushed them all along lately. And it had been in just the right direction.

The End

ABOUT THE AUTHOR

Having spent far too much time hopping from subject to subject at university, back in her native country of Sweden, Emma finally emerged with a degree in Library and Information Science.

She now lives with her wife and two cats in England. There is no point in saying which city, as they move about once a year. She spends her free time writing, reading, daydreaming, working out, and watching whichever television show has the most lesbian subtext at the time.

Her tastes in most things usually lean towards the quirky and she loves genres like urban fantasy, magic realism, and steampunk.

Emma is also a hopeless sap for any small chubby creature with tiny legs, and can often be found making heart-eyes at things like guinea pigs, wombats, marmots, and human toddlers.

You can connect with Emma at www.writingradleys.com

COMING SOON FROM HEARTSOME BOOKS

HUNTRESS

A.E. RADLEY

Amy is stuck in a rut. After graduating, she never left her temporary job at the motorway service station. Daily visits from a mysterious woman are the highlight of her days.

Until one day, when the mystery woman vanishes.

Amy investigates the disappearance and makes a shocking discovery. Suddenly, she's being framed and no-nonsense Claudia McAllister is being sent to arrest her.

Will Amy's unique approach to evading capture prove successful?

HEARTSOMEBOOKS.COM

COMING SOON FROM HEARTSOME BOOKS

THE LOUDEST SILENCE

OLIVIA JANAE

Kate, an up and coming cellist, is new to Chicago and the 'Windy City Chamber Ensemble'. During her first rehearsal, she is surprised and intrigued to meet Vivian Kensington, the formidable by reputation board president who also happens to be...deaf.

Slowly Kate develops a tentative friendship with the cold-hearted woman and as she does, she finds a kindness and a warmth that she never expected.

As their friendship begins to grow into something more, Kate wonders, is it possible for two women, one from a world of sound and one a world of silence, to truly understand one another?

HEARTSOMEBOOKS**.COM**

70552307R00087

Made in the USA
Columbia, SC
09 May 2017